celg

W9-DCA-107

DEADWOOD
AMBUSH

Center Point
Large Print

Also by Lauran Paine and available from
Center Point Large Print:

Kansas Kid
Night of the Rustler's Moon
Wagon Train West
Iron Marshal
Six-Gun Crossroads
Prairie Town
Dead Man's Cañon
Lightning Strike
Reckoning at Lansing's Ferry
The Drifter
Trail of Shadows
Winter Moon
The Texan Rides Alone
Terror in Gunsight
The Story of Buckhorn
Renegades of Perdition Range
Absaroka Valley
Cheyenne Pass

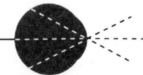

**This Large Print Book carries the
Seal of Approval of N.A.V.H.**

DEADWOOD AMBUSH

LAURAN PAINE

CENTER POINT LARGE PRINT
THORNDIKE, MAINE

This Center Point Large Print edition
is published in the year 2020 in co-operation with
Golden West Literary Agency.

February 2020
First Edition

Printed in the United States of America
on permanent paper.
Set in 16-point Times New Roman type.

ISBN: 978-1-64358-507-9

The Library of Congress has cataloged this record
under Library of Congress Control Number: 2019952043

DEADWOOD AMBUSH

CHAPTER ONE

The land was broken and buckled. There were mining camps, freighter camps, and cow camps scattered across it. There were also Indian camps, but these were few and beggarly, louse-infested in appearance and also in actuality.

Deadwood was a tent town. It was summer now, therefore the broad central roadway was ankle-deep in gritty dust, but in the early spring, the fall, and often too in the dead of the blizzardly winters when Chinook winds came to thaw things out, the roadway was a morass of black mud, and ruts knee-deep to a tall mule.

Deadwood had law, of a kind, the same as it had ethics and standards, of a kind. If a drunken miner or cowboy wished to brawl, there were always plenty of like-souls handy to furnish brawny opposition. The law seldom interfered. Murders being commonplace, there were just too many for one lawman to solve, or even to adequately investigate. Robberies likewise. Robberies were so frequent, so almost casual in commission day and night, that unless the victim lost a considerable amount of money—cash or gold dust—he seldom even bothered to file a complaint because, under the annoyed eye of Marshal Fred Nolan and his two deputy marshals,

Wentworth and Grubb, the victim could feel the gloom, the disapproval, the antagonism building up around him like a solid wall.

But if the gold rush had inundated Deadwood with rabble, with gunfighters, gamblers, fast women, and slow freights, it had also brought with it a share, too, of men whose earlier environments had inculcated them with at least an aversion to blatant crime and open hostility to decency, if not necessarily any great degree of piety or straight-laced morality. The odd thing about this, too, was that a good deal of decency was found in the least likely places.

The notorious Texas gunman Ben Thompson, for instance, decided one night crooked gamblers were too common in Deadwood, had a warming drink at a bar, and proceeded to tree the town with his six-gun and thin out the ranks of dishonest card players. Ben was fined very moderately the following morning and admonished. That was the end of it for both Ben and the light-fingered fraternity. Ben left Deadwood and the gamblers came out of hiding.

The affair which briefly held the spotlight in Deadwood two weeks after Ben Thompson's departure, was more sanguine. At least its overtones did not blink out quite so readily as happened with Ben Thompson's episode. But then, with Ben there had been no personal injury involved, as there was in the subsequent affair.

People in Deadwood had a free and easy manner; it wasn't necessary to be introduced to a man to speak to him, and if names were used at all they frequently were derived from some characteristic others noticed, much as the Indians named others. For example, there was a crippled youth of perhaps seventeen or eighteen years of age whose badly broken and badly re-set left leg gave him a peculiar crab-like sideward gait. The rough miners and stockmen called this youth Hopalong or Gitalong or Limpy, whatever name popped into their minds at the time, but each name indicative of his crippled condition.

No one knew anything about Gitalong and no one cared. Deadwood had its share of roving youths, mostly runaway and parentless, some good, some middling-to-fair, and a lot just plain ornery. Gitalong belonged to the first or second category as far as anyone knew. He lived in a low-roofed, unsteady lean-to he'd cobbled together out of broken planks, cast-off wagon canvasses, and soiled sacking. He did laundry, ran errands, and when business was poor in these lines of endeavor, he could usually be found outside Ace Morton's Bluebell Saloon hopefully waiting for someone to dash up on a lathered horse, which he'd offer to "cool-out" for a dime, or maybe take across to the livery barn for a five-cent piece.

Gitalong was a hustler. He was also a familiar

sight around Deadwood, summer or winter, in his oversized hand-me-down cast-off clothing, his cracked boots, and his warped left leg. People recognized him like they also recognized the permanence of the Black Hills roundabout, or the evening stage, or the everlasting summertime dust—as something familiar and acceptable and totally unimportant.

Gitalong was tall. He was also thin. It was this thinness which made him seem even taller. At six feet in height he didn't weigh over a hundred and thirty-five pounds wringing wet. Or, as Marshal Fred Nolan had sagely observed one time, Gitalong was skinny enough to drop through the hole in the seat of his pants and choke himself to death.

He was outside the Bluebell the bright, sun-shiny morning when three dusted-over trail hands hit town from a new cow camp westerly near the river where one of the northbound Montana herds had bedded down the evening before. There were two other strangers tying up at the rack, granite-jawed, gray-eyed, taciturn men, also dusted over. Gitalong had hit these first two up to walk their animals or run errands for them. They had both gazed at him, up and down, and had shaken their heads, so he now turned to the three young buckaroos with the same offer.

One of the cowboys rolled his eyes around at the other two as he swung down, and broadly smiled as he said in his unmistakable Texas drawl: "Well, sir, ole busted laig, there *is* an errand you could run for me and my pardners. Now tell me, right out now, ole gimpy, how much do you charge for these here errands you run fer folks?"

Gitalong's very thin face smiled back at the husky range rider. "Dime," he said, "for any errand here in town. Just a dime."

The drover dug in a trouser pocket, came up with a small silver coin, and looked around as the other two swaggered up, their eyes bright with mischief. He looked back at Gitalong still grinning, but with his eyelids drooping just a little.

"Here's the dime, crippled boy. Now all you got to do is run and fetch us three girls. That's all." The Texan pushed out his hand. "Take it, ole busted laig, it's your dime. Take it."

Gitalong looked at the outheld hand. He looked into the husky cowboy's grinning face and unsmiling, scornful eyes.

"I can't do that," he said, reddening. "I run other kind of errands."

The cowboy drew back his hand, his smile dying. "You can't or you won't?" he asked. "Ole busted laig, where we come from when a fellow tells a fellow like you to jump . . . all you do is ask how high. Now you better go fetch them girls, 'cause I got a feelin' under them rags you're wearin' you need a bath, and yonder's a big ole waterin' trough."

Gitalong's dark-ringed gray gaze turned apprehensive. He was cornered; he couldn't out-run them and he couldn't out-fight them. He'd been bullied before. He knew exactly what was going to happen now, too, and afterward, when he crawled out of the trough, everyone would roar with laughter. He swallowed painfully.

"Well, ole busted laig," asked the burly Texan in his menacingly soft drawl. "How about it . . . you want the dime . . . or the dunkin'?"

Across the tie rack one of those other strangers, a man in his middle thirties somewhere, thick and muscled-up and thin-lipped, leaned over the pole, looked at those three drovers, and said: "Cowboy, you've already had a dime's worth of fun with him, so maybe you better just hand it over. And if you want some more fun with him, seems to me it ought to be worth maybe a dime a half hour, or somethin' like that."

Gitalong's head jerked around. Those three Texas drovers only had to shift their eyes to see that leaning, dusty man at the rack. He was alone; at least as far as they saw right then, he was alone. They studied him carefully because his stare and his voice, even his choice of words, told them this was no one to fool with. Still, they were three and he was just one man.

The husky rider deliberately put that dime into

his trouser pocket without taking his eyes off the stranger near the end of Ace Morton's hitch rack. He didn't say anything, just pocketed the coin and stared. The men on either side of him also stared. They knew a dozen different ways to make someone who butted into their business wish he hadn't, especially with odds like three to one. They stood easy, hands resting lightly upon hip-holstered .45s, and waited. This was their friend's game; they'd let him set the openers.

The older man straightened up off the rack but kept his thick left hand lying atop it. His right hand was hanging straight down with the gently curled fingers within inches of a black-butted .45 in a flesh-out holster.

"Reckon you don't hear good, Texas," he said to the husky drover. "But I'm a patient fellow, so I'll try once more. Give the lad that dime you just pocketed."

"You figure to make me do that, mister?" drawled the husky Texan, his eyes turning very bright and dry.

The older man looked at all three of those drovers. His nearly lipless wide mouth faintly curled at its outer corners.

"Tough and rough and wild and woolly," he said quietly, and nodded his head. That nod was the signal.

From behind the Texans a naked six-gun rose and fell, rose and fell. The dangerous-eyed Texan gave a little start as both his friends crumpled without a sound. He spun around, his right hand moving. A .45 hit him hard in the soft parts making him gasp and flinch and drop the gun he'd partially drawn, back into its holster. That other stranger was behind the gun in his middle as the drover straightened up.

Behind him a voice said: "The dime, Texas, give this fellow his dime. On second thought, since three of us were involved here, maybe you'd better raise that ante a mite. My pardner and I don't work for chicken feed, so maybe you better fork over three silver dollars, Texas."

The silent, impassive-faced man holding his six-gun gave it a vicious dig. The Texan gasped again, ran a hand into one pocket, and came up with three silver dollars which he held out.

"Turn around," ordered the man at the hitch rack. "Fine. Now hand that three dollars to the crippled lad." When this had been done the stranger behind the drover put up his six-gun, gave the Texan a rough shove, stepped over an unconscious man, and strolled on over to join his friend leaning upon the rack. Throughout the entire interlude this man had not uttered a sound.

Gitalong, with those three big cartwheels in his hand, stood dumbfoundedly gazing down at the crumpled Texans. Each of them had been fortunate—wearing hats minimized the danger of gun-barrel cuts, or even concussion, which could

14

be fatal. He looked around at the two older men. They were simply looking on now, waiting for the Texan to do something.

Gitalong pocketed the money, made squiggly marks in the dust as he dragged his warped leg over to help one of those knocked-out men groan his way back to consciousness and get unsteadily upright. The husky drover got his other friend upon his feet, too, but this one was slower coming round. He had to be supported and vigorously shaken before his eyes flickered.

The spokesman for those three turned upon that pair of impassive older men farther down the rack.

"Had to slip in behind us to do it," he snarled. "All right, granger, you asked for it. There are seven more of us down along the river."

The drover Gitalong was aiding shook him off and wrinkled his nose at the boy. "Man, Reb wasn't just funnin'. You sure-Lord *do* need a dunkin' in some water."

Gitalong turned red and stepped away as this drover picked up his hat, looked around, set the hat gingerly atop his head.

"Reb, what in tarnation happened?" the drover asked one of his partners.

The one called Reb growled: "Never mind. Gimme a hand gettin' Charley atop his danged horse. We're headin' back to camp. Then we're comin' back. Come on . . . don't stand there battin' your danged eyes and feelin' your head. Gimme a hand here."

Gitalong edged over closer to those lounging strangers at the rack. Men were passing back and forth upon the plank walk behind them. There were wagons and riders out in the dazzling roadway as well, but if anyone looked, all they saw was two unsteady drovers heaving a third unsteady drover across his saddle in front of Ace Morton's Bluebell Saloon. Even in early morning this was not unusual in Deadwood, Dakota Territory.

CHAPTER TWO

Gitalong's palm was damp from clutching those three silver dollars. He hoisted himself around to watch Reb and his headachy friends rein away from the hitch rack and start back out of town. He turned around, all the way around, and saw that neither of those rough, older men were there. He thought he spotted the silent one just passing on into Morton's saloon. He wanted to give those men the three dollars. Maybe they had no right to it, but neither did he, and he had a knot of fear in his belly. Those Texans would be back. Like they threatened, they'd be back with more of their same kind along, which spelled trouble.

He was not allowed inside the Bluebell Saloon though. Black-eyed, merciless Ace Morton had himself laid down that edict. No tramps or beggars or misfits allowed in his bar. Gitalong had no difficultly recalling the evening last spring when Ace Morton had clubbed him alongside the ear, had dragged him outside, and had flung him bodily under the horses at the hitch rack. If it hadn't been for a bearded big moose of a freighter in a checkered wool shirt, Gitalong might have been stamped or kicked to death by those frightened horses. As the freighter quieted the horses, waded in, and saved him, black-eyed Ace had stood up there in front of his spindle doors and had laid down the law.

"No damned cripples or beggars allowed in the Bluebell. You better remember that, you stinkin' cripple, because next time I'll stomp on your good leg!"

Gitalong remembered it vividly.

Now he turned and started on over toward the livery barn. Traffic was becoming heavy, near midday. It followed no pattern and was motivated by only two considerations: getting where it was bound and avoiding any serious collision which might prevent it from getting there. Frail human bodies were not considered likely to produce delaying results, so freighters, miners, wagoneers of every description, and even the muleback and horseback riders, paid no heed at all to a crab-gaited ragged wraith of a six-foot-tall wisp of a man-boy.

But Gitalong was experienced. He'd been making this perilous crossing for almost two years now. He got across in front of the livery barn, got up onto the rough boardwalk, and had then only to work his way through the pedestrians, who were almost exclusively masculine, and also almost always burdened with something—a hundredweight of sacked flour or meal upon brawny shoulders, boxes or tools or packages. Everyone was in a hurry. Everyone was swiftly moving along toward some private rendezvous with destiny which, in ninety-five percent of the cases, was ultimate discouragement in the mines or the placer diggings.

There was a hearty big youth who cuffed horses for the livery man named Jeremiah Perkins. Jeremiah was a runaway. He was also a booming-voiced, iron-hided lad the same age as Gitalong, who sometimes was friendly and sometimes was brusque, depending upon the amount of work ahead of him, and his mood. But Jeremiah, for some reason he never bothered to explain—and refused to even admit to himself because to pity someone was to be weak and unmanly—was usually approachable.

When Gitalong came dragging his crooked leg through the livery barn dust to show Jeremiah that three dollars, Perkins's eyebrows shot straight up and his eyes, pale blue, got very round.

"You stole it," he pronounced. "Gitalong, the danged law will be all over you like a rash."

Gitalong told how he'd come by the money. Jeremiah listened and scowled, and eventually shook his head.

"Them cussed cowboys will come back huntin' you," he said. "If I was in your boots, I'd scuttle into your shack and lie low until the herd pulls out."

"What I want," explained Gitalong, "is for someone to give this money back to those cowboys. Or to those two strangers who kept me from getting flung in the trough. They're up at . . ."

"Me?" boomed Jeremiah Perkins, gripping his manure fork in both hands. "Gitalong, you askin' *me* to give that money back?"

"Mister Morton won't allow me in his saloon, Jeremiah. Otherwise I'd do it."

"You're crazy," growled the larger, thicker youth. "Keep the three bucks. Go hole up in your shack. Them Texans will never find you there. Then, when they pull out tomorrow or the next day . . . you got three whole dollars."

A beer-barrel shaped man up near the roadway entrance roared hair-raisingly down the runway in a voice that made every wall shake. He was addressing Perkins, and Jeremiah at once turned to rush away.

"I got to get back to work now," he told Gitalong. "See you later."

For Gitalong there was no other place to go, unless it was to his lean-to shack. Not everyone in Deadwood scorned him, but those who didn't had their own problems or else they were too busy to be bothered listening to him. Deadwood was a busy place by day and a wildly, frantically busy place by night. He shrugged and limped along to his shack. One thing Jeremiah Perkins had said which was true was that those drovers wouldn't find him in his shack. Another thing which Jeremiah had also said which was probably true was that those herders would move out in a day or two. Stock feed for five miles in any direction from Deadwood was very poor. On top of that, there were just enough desperate and destitute men skulking the countryside hungrily awaiting an opportunity to slit a critter's throat in the dark to make keeping a herd of cattle safe a near impossibility.

There had of course been a few lynchings as a result of this kind of depredation, but folks' hearts weren't really in it even as they hauled on the hang ropes. This land was bountifully good to the fortunate few. To the others, it was degradingly harsh and merciless. Still, the reasoning went, unless crime was punished it would increase and flourish even more than it already did. As U.S. Marshal Fred Nolan told a pair of quiet strangers in Ace Morton's place the evening of the same day Gitalong acquired his three silver cartwheels: "Sometimes the law's got to compromise a little and maybe overlook the fact that lynching's not exactly legal, because otherwise, if the miners and stockmen get discouraged, they won't help the law at all, you see."

What Gitalong wondered about as he hunched down to crawl into his gloomy lean-to, was just how determined those drovers might be, because if they were *real* determined, Jeremiah would be wrong. They'd find him, and of course if they did, this time it wouldn't be just a dunking in the public trough.

He had some jerky in an old parfleche bag he'd bought off a drunken Indian. Originally there'd been about fifty pounds of this dried, gnarled venison but now there wasn't more than perhaps five or six pounds left. He was tired of jerky three times a day anyway. It was much better than going hungry, but with three silver dollars he could walk right up to the counter down at the emporium and buy four tins of ham or a half barrel of salt pork.

He ate jerky.

Evening came and with it Gitalong's uneasiness increased. He had no idea where, down along the westerly river, those drovers had their camp, but he *did* know, because he knew the Deadwood countryside, that enough time had elapsed for those three angry riders to get back to their camp, relate what had happened, round up their friends, and start back for town.

There was a girl. Her father ran the saddle and harness shop. Her name was Bedelia Wilson but folks called her Delia. She pitied Gitalong. From time to time when they'd meet she'd talk to him, smile at him, and if this didn't do much for his masculine pride because he knew perfectly well why she did it, still, even the pity of a pretty girl like Delia Wilson was better than being ignored.

It occurred to him to seek her now, explain what had happened, and let her keep the three silver dollars.

That wasn't his only reason for seeking her. He was honest enough with himself to admit this too. Whenever life seemed near to suffocating Gitalong, he'd go and talk with Delia. He didn't recall his own mother, had no idea whether he'd had any brothers or sisters, but he did know, because he'd had many black and lonely nights to dwell upon it, that everyone needs someone else, and he needed Delia.

He finished his skimpy supper, crawled back out of the lean-to, stood up to beat dirt from his ragged clothing, sniffed the lowering night, listened to the town's evening noises, and started southward down through back lots where refuse lay in random piles, bound for the saddle and harness shop. He had the three dollars in a pocket.

Marshal Nolan's two deputies, Bill Wentworth and Al Grubb, were across the road in front of the stage company office idling away time with smokes and small talk when Gitalong glided forth from between two shacks and emerged onto the rough boardwalk north of Wilson's harness works.

Bill Wentworth, former range rider, six feet tall, and about a hundred and seventy-five pounds worth of muscle and sinew, exhaled a cloud of blue smoke. He looked at his fellow deputy and said: "Al, yonder's that rag-pickin' kid who's got the shack out back of the livery barn. You know, except for bein' starved down to a shadow and havin' that crooked leg, he's not a bad-lookin' fellow."

Deputy Grubb, shorter, blockier, black-eyed, dark-haired, scarred from many fights, and somewhat beetle-browed, gazed across the road dispassionately. Grubb could feel sorry for someone like Gitalong. He was as hard and unflinching as rock, but he wasn't entirely without feelings. Still, since coming to Deadwood and starving out in the diggings before he took the job with Marshal Nolan, he'd seen so much hardship and suffering he'd turned calloused. Now he simply gazed over where Gitalong was moving southward toward the lighted harness shop window with his peculiar, crab-like gait, and said: "Bill, one of these winters we'll get called to go down there, burn his shack, and bury him, 'cause he done froze in his sleep. Where'd he come from, anyway?"

Wentworth dropped his cigarette and stepped on it. "Who knows? Who knows where any of 'em came from? Who cares? They strike it rich or they don't. They stick around cuttin' a big sashay if they strike pay dirt . . . or one mornin' they're gone back to wherever they come from."

"Or," added Al Grubb, "they got no way of

gettin' back and they turn to stickin' up stages or miners or they maybe go into the rustlin' business . . . and wind up dead."

Wentworth, with nothing better to hold his interest, watched Gitalong peer into the saddle-shop window, go to the roadside door, hesitate long enough to push his filthy old shirt into his trousers, reach for the latch string, and walk on in.

"Goin' to buy himself a new saddle," the taller of the two deputies said facetiously, and wagged his head. "What's ahead for a lad like Gitalong?"

Grubb didn't answer. This was the supper hour and Deadwood was quiet for a change, but it wouldn't remain this way for long. Soon now, the drovers and miners, the freighters and townsmen, would be heading for their favorite saloons or variety houses and the entire tempo of Deadwood would subtly change. After that, Grubb and Wentworth would be busy stopping fights, jailing obstreperous drunks, intervening between fired-up, gun-wearing battlers, and before dawn they'd also have to haul a corpse or two down to the embalming shed behind Fred Nolan's jailhouse. The days were not always the same, but the nights were.

Wentworth, too, dropped the subject of Gitalong. "There's a fresh band of Texas drovers southward down the river," he said, sounding resigned about this. "Saw their camp on my way back from huntin' loose horses this afternoon. The herd's fair sized . . . maybe a thousand head."

"Montana bound," stated Al Grubb, making a statement of this even though he didn't know this was true at all. "They're all Montana bound this time of year. I wish to hell they'd find some other route and by-pass Deadwood. These smelly miners are bad enough, but cowboys coming in after six weeks on the trail are like a keg of gunpowder with a short fuse."

"Looked like a Texas outfit," put in Bill Wentworth. "I didn't talk to them but I saw three of them comin' back from town. They was lollin' in the saddle like they had a snoot full, and their outfits were pure Texas."

"The worst kind," pronounced burly Al Grubb, gazing northward up toward Ace Morton's Bluebell Saloon and sounding funereal about this. "What is it that makes Texans so dog-goned troublesome all the time? Remember Ben Thompson?"

Wentworth nodded. He remembered all right. Ben had forced him to dive under one of Morton's poker tables, that night he erupted up there.

"But Ben was different. He was a professional. Mostly, these drovers are just average cowboys."

"Humph," grunted Grubb disparagingly. "No such thing as an 'average' cowboy. You shake any ten of 'em until their teeth rattle loose, and nine times out of ten bullets will fall out. Especially these drovers. They're wanted somewhere . . . down in Texas maybe, or up in Kansas. Joinin' a trail drive gives 'em a real good excuse for hightailin' it. No, sir, Bill, never make the mistake of figurin' drovers are just average cowboys. Especially don't make that mistake when your back's turned to 'em."

"Fred's coming," said Deputy Marshal Wentworth, and jutted his chin toward the striding shadow of a solidly made six-footer walking southward down the sidewalk toward them. "Had his supper. Now maybe we can get ours."

Nolan was a capable, shrewd, and tough man, compactly put together. He had light eyes and dark hair and looked to be in his middle thirties although there were crow's feet wrinkles up around his observant eyes that made him seem older. He veered over at sight of his deputies and halted.

"Ought to be an interesting night in town," he said blandly, gazing away from Grubb's dour features to Wentworth's less grumpy expression. "Some Texas riders got a camp down along the river."

"Yeah, we know," responded Bill Wentworth.

"How many?" asked Grubb.

"Ten. At least that's the number I heard up at Morton's place," Nolan replied. "I also heard something else up there. Seems three of 'em hit town earlier and started out to roust Gitalong a little, and a brace of strangers knocked two of 'em over the head and buffaloed the third one."

Al Grub looked around. "Why?" he asked.

"Well, I just told you," stated the marshal. "For hoorawing Gitalong."

Grubb kept gazing at Nolan. A little hoorawing never hurt anyone. Besides, everyone teased Gitalong. It wasn't anything to get feisty about. Still, you couldn't ever be sure how folks would react to things. Al shrugged and turned back to leaning there and gazing up the darkened roadway.

There were lights at the livery barn, at Morton's bar, along the roadway here and there. Squares of orange brightness lay down across the plank walk and out into the manured broad roadway. The supper hour quietude was beginning to dissolve. Walking miners began filtering into town from the roundabout diggings. Over at the livery barn Jeremiah Perkins came out to take charge of a team and wagon as nearly a dozen rough men jumped down and noisily stamped around, speaking back and forth. Deadwood's night life was about to quicken.

Southward of the livery barn where there was a hutment café—boarded halfway up with planking, but roofed over with a wagon-canvas top—two men strolled out into the pleasant evening to stand loosely upon the edge of the walkway. One of them had a toothpick drooping from his lips. The other one was smoking a brown-paper cigarette. In build they were very similar. In personalities, too, they seemed alike, for although they spoke back and forth now and then, the conversation never appeared to consist of more than a sentence at a time. They watched those miners up in front of the livery barn, and when the miners left, walking purposefully toward the Bluebell Saloon, and seven mounted drovers rode up all in a quiet bunch at the livery barn, those two strangers also watched them. But now they stopped casually speaking back and forth.

CHAPTER THREE

Marshal Nolan and his pair of deputies had no inkling there was anything wrong until one of those drovers up in front of the livery barn looked southward, down in front of the hutment café, and said something to the two riders closest to him. Those two stepped up out of the livery barn's lights and stared southward too. One of them started walking ahead in an unmistakable manner, stiff-legged and jerky.

"Hey," Nolan breathed suddenly. "Look yonder. That's the Texas drovers sure as shooting and one of 'em's on the peck already."

Deputy Al Grubb straightened up off the post he'd been leaning upon. He spat out a crisp oath. "Headin' for those two fellows in front of the café," he informed them. "Let's go."

The three of them stepped forth into the roadway and began walking diagonally across through the thin night-time traffic.

The other drovers called questions over where that angry man was walking. He didn't answer but those other two men did.

"Them's the pair that buffaloed us," one of them growled.

The cowboys peered southward through evening's settled gloom. They saw the pair of silent, waiting men in front of the café. They didn't see the converging law officers, not right away.

Someone over in that group said cheerfully: "Well, let's get back the three dollars, then go drink it up."

All the rest of those drovers started down toward the pair of motionless strangers in front of the restaurant. At first, there was no attitude of trouble among the Texans. The cowboy who had already started southward down the roadway though, was different. He was set for trouble, primed to fight, had his right arm hooked the slightest bit at the elbow and his dead-level gaze intently watchful.

The pair of men outside the café hadn't moved. Evidently they had not expected this situation to develop, or at least not so suddenly. The one with the smoke dropped it and freed both his hands. The one chewing upon the toothpick went right on chewing.

No one, least of all Marshal Fred Nolan or his deputies, saw the crab-gaited scarecrow come scuttling northward up the plank walk from Wilson's harness works, but even if Gitalong had been noticed no one would have paid him the slightest heed now. The business at hand was lethal, had nothing to do with a harmless cripple, and claimed the undivided attention of all those converging men.

Up at Morton's saloon the music began. A number of men with cracked voices began singing. Other riders were coming into town now too and even the number of pedestrians began to increase as Deadwood's night life took over.

That cold-eyed drover who'd started toward the café first got in front of the pair of quiet strangers upon the plank walk's edge, and halted. The three of them exchanged looks. From the middle of the roadway Marshal Nolan couldn't see the Texan's face, only his back. Also, it was too dark under the yonder overhang to make out the faces of the two stocky men he was facing. But Fred Nolan had no misgivings. He and Al and Bill weren't more than fifty feet off. The other Texans saw them coming, finally. Saw the dull shine of their badges, and slowed a little, milled around as uncertain men oftentimes do.

The drover out in the roadway said something. Nolan heard the growl of low words over the other night-time sounds but he had no idea what was said. One of those men upon the plank walk spoke back and Nolan heard what this one said.

"Back off, buster. You asked for, you got it, and that's the end of it. Now run along before you get your britches paddled."

There hadn't been even a hint of fear in that stocky man's voice, which seemed unusual to

Marshal Nolan, because those two strangers couldn't help but realize all those other drovers were only a short distance northward of them.

The Texas drover went for his gun. Nolan saw that as plain as day. So did Al Grubb and Bill Wentworth. But just ahead of that, the two strangers upon the plank walk moved. It was almost as though the drover had given them some kind of a signal. One of them stepped wide sideways. The other one simply dropped down to one knee. It was this one that fired simultaneously with the Texan.

Nolan, Wentworth, and Grubb, directly behind that Texan, had scarcely a fraction of a second's warning. Still they managed to lunge sideways to get clear.

Al Grubb ripped out a furious and startled curse.

The kneeling man fired again, but the Texan was already falling when the second slug hit him. All it did was hasten his collapse.

The standing stranger swung his gun on the dumbfounded drovers northward. He didn't say a word, just held that cocked .45 on them and waited.

It was the astonishment of this sudden killing that had the other cowboys off balance. Marshal Nolan, experienced in these things, jumped into the breach by throwing down on the Texans also. A fraction of a second later Wentworth and Grubb also threw down on them. If any of the Texans, when their shock passed, thought of retaliation, the notion passed as those three obviously capable law officers stepped on up and faced them.

Marshal Nolan said: "You boys better pick up your friend there in the road and get on out of town. Don't come back until daylight, and if you've got some notion of treein' the town about this, don't try that either because we've got two shotguns for every man-jack of you."

The strangers in front of the café were side by side again, facing northward. Across the road men came tumbling out of dark places to see what the shooting had been about. Up at the Bluebell Saloon, a band of half-drunk miners and townsmen came boiling out into the speckle-lighted roadway. No one, though, hastened southward where there were still five drawn guns wickedly reflecting light. Men cat-called profane questions back and forth.

One of those Texans, a bull-necked, pock-marked man with pale eyes nearly hidden behind the perpetual droop of thick lids, shoved both thumbs into his shell belt, gazed at his dead cowboy out there, gazed southward where those two stocky strangers still stood, and finally lifted his glance to Marshal Nolan.

"That," he pronounced, "was murder, Sheriff. Plain and simple murder, Sheriff."

"Murder my foot," contradicted beetle-browed Al Grubb. "We saw it too, mister. Your cowboy went for his gun first."

Nolan made a curt gesture toward Grubb, ordering him to be silent. "I'm a U.S. marshal, not a sheriff," said Nolan, "and if that was murder, mister, then I never saw a fair fight before. Now take your friend out of town and bury him, or if we have to do it for you, the town will levy a slight charge."

The Texans came out of their shock gradually. They looked at one another and over where Nolan, Wentworth, and Grubb stood, still with their guns drawn. Several of them muttered. The thick-necked, narrow-eyed drover made a long, careful study of Marshal Nolan.

"You goin' to convene an inquest, Marshal?" he asked finally, his eyes piercing the lawman.

Nolan nodded. "We always do in cases like this."

"And how many witnesses you got that'll swear this was a shoot-out?"

"Three peace officers and those two fellows who were involved," retorted Fred Nolan.

The Texan slowly wagged his head back and forth. "Ain't enough," he growled. "Ain't nowhere near enough, Marshal. There's six of us right here'll swear that stranger over there done shot and deliberately murdered my rider." Slowly the Texan rocked back on his booted heels, his expression turning crafty. "By morning, Marshal, I'll have fifty more witnesses, too. Figure to pick up at least that many in the saloons around town. What kind of a decision will your inquest jury bring in then, Marshal?"

Al Grubb started to snarl a hot retort to this, but one of those two strangers farther back stepped up and holstered his six-gun as he said: "That'll work in Texas, but not in Dakota Territory, cowboy, so let me give you a little advice. Before any more of you boys get hurt, go on back to your camp and cool off. We weren't huntin' trouble. We still aren't. If your man hadn't thought he had big Texas odds . . . seven to two . . . he'd be alive right now."

One of the Texans replied bitterly: "For a lousy three dollars."

The others were silent. They studied that blocky man with the holstered gun. They hadn't seen him draw and fire; they'd only seen him drop down so that their friend's bullet went over his head, but that was enough, for they too were seasoned frontier fighting men. This stranger, whoever he was, knew the tricks, the ruses, the ways of survival.

Marshal Nolan put up his weapon. Bill Wentworth also did, but Al Grubb, less trusting, only lowered his. That other stranger back there in the shadows swept back his coat, dropped his .45 into its holster, and stepped over to gaze down into the still, gray face of the dead Texan. He had nothing to say.

"Well," demanded Nolan of the bull-necked Texan, "what'll it be . . . you fellows plant him and save two dollars, or we bury him here and you pay the two dollars?"

"You'll play hell gettin' two dollars out of me," snarled the Texan. "Even if you had to plant him, you wouldn't get it. Boys, pick Reb up and tie him across his saddle."

Several men ambled over to bend and lifted up the dead man. For as long as this held everyone's attention there was nothing more said. Along both plank walks men clustered darkly. Even out in the center of the roadway they stood watching quietly. It was a large crowd, and here and there in it were drunks who kept calling out garrulous questions or pithy comments, but down in front of the hutment café none of this was particularly heeded.

When the corpse had been taken back up to the livery barn by all but one or two of the drovers, the bull-necked spokesman for the Texans said to Marshal Nolan: "Earlier today those two fellows robbed that dead man of three dollars in silver. That's what we come to town to see about. Now you got robbery *and* murder, Marshal. I want those two men locked up as robbers." He pointed ahead where the pair of strangers was quietly standing.

Fred Nolan nodded without taking his eyes off the Texans. "We'll investigate," he replied. "We'll do it *after* you boys leave Deadwood."

Out of the southward gloom Gitalong hunched forward, dragging his crooked leg and holding out his bony right hand. "Here's the money," he breathlessly said, making straight for that beefy Texan. "I wanted to give it back. I honestly did, mister." Keeping his distance, Gitalong stopped, still holding out his hand with the silver dollars.

The Texan gazed at him through his narrowed eyes. He looked Gitalong up and down. His lip curled in scorn. "Yeah, you wanted to give it back," he said softly. "Why didn't you hand it over before my men left town, you stinkin' cripple, you?" With a blur of striking speed the burly man struck Gitalong's hand, knocking the silver dollars out into the dark roadway.

In a second, battle-scarred Al Grubb was moving. He got past Nolan's swiftly outflung arm with a low and deep-down growl and lunged at the other thick-set man. The Texan tried to twist quickly enough to meet this abrupt attack and only half made it. Grubb had the Texan by the shirt front, his powerful shoulders rolling up as he inexorably pulled the other man's face to within inches of his own.

Grubb called the Texan a fighting name, his little eyes smoldering with combative urge. "The kid don't lie," he said. "But even if he was lyin'

. . . this town doesn't need Texans. So pick up your lousy three dollars, cowboy, and clear out of here!"

Grubb let that sink in, then gave the burly drover a violent backward shove and instantly dropped his right hand straight downward. The Texan had no chance. By the time he caught his balance again, Bill Wentworth and Marshal Nolan were also closely watching him, their gun hands also positioned to draw and fire.

Those other drovers, sensing a renewal of hostilities, began walking back down toward their spokesman again, walking stiff-legged and willing, their coats brushed back, their hip-holstered guns exposed and instantly available.

"Steady," said one of the strangers in front of the café. "You there . . . crippled boy . . . get out of the way!"

Gitalong hitched himself over against a wooden wall and stiffened there, scarcely breathing, scarcely daring to even roll his eyes around.

"Git!" ordered Al Grubb, glaring straight at the bull-necked drover. "Get your crew mounted up and git!"

Fred Nolan, angry at his deputy, nevertheless concentrated upon the bull-necked man.

"Do like he says, mister," Nolan softly said. "And like I said before . . . don't come back to Deadwood until you've cooled off. Not until broad daylight."

The Texans, with that big crowd of onlooking, rough men out in the roadway darkly muttering against them, too, had no alternative. They went up to their horses, got astride, turned, and looked out over Deadwood, waiting for their spokesman to lead them back westward, seething as they did so. They were rough men, every one of them. They had treed their share of towns and they'd even shot up a few, too, but never before had they been run out like this, when there were seven of them, all armed and mounted. Whatever came out of this, one thing was certain: not a man among those Texans would ever forget Deadwood, Dakota Territory.

The bull-necked man settled across leather and switched his attention from Marshal Nolan to Al Grubb. To Al he said: "Mister, ain't a livin' man roughs me up like that without us settlin' it later."

"Aw," snarled Grubb, his thick, bushy brows dropping low like the dark wings of a bird, "go make your big brag somewhere else, Texas. Deadwood's seen a hundred just like you come and go. Beat it . . . go on now . . . ride out of town."

The Texans rode slowly away. Out in the roadway several drunks threw profane taunts after them. The crowd began to break up, to go back to the bars and poker tables. Men hooted after the horsemen, laughing at them in rough contempt. Deadwood had no more use for men who were backed down than any other frontier town had, but the difference here was simply that these were Texans who had been backed down, and whether the miners realized it yet or not, *that* made a difference.

CHAPTER FOUR

"Where in hell did that three dollars go?" muttered Bill Wentworth as he scuffed out in the roadway seeking the money. No one paid him much attention. Over in front of the hutment café where Gitalong rigidly stood, looking ghost-like in the feeble light, Fred Nolan was having a conversation with the two strangers. It had to do with how this entire affair with the Texans had got its start. The two were brothers, Con and Ez Wheeler, and it was Con, the one who had killed the Texan called Reb, that told Nolan about the earlier meeting with those three bullying Texans. Ez Wheeler stood back near Gitalong thoughtfully rolling himself a smoke. He had nothing at all to say. When he lighted up, he gazed straight at Gitalong through the quick, hot sputter of the match's flare, and he smiled.

"Nothing to sweat about now, kid," Ez Wheeler said. "They're gone, and when the deputy finds your money, he'll give it back to you."

Gitalong said swiftly, almost breathlessly: "I don't want the money back. I didn't want any of this to happen. That's what I was trying to do this afternoon . . . get rid of that money. Give it to you . . . to anyone who'd take it."

Ez Wheeler gazed from the glowing tip of his

smoke to Gitalong. Behind him Al Grubb and Fred Nolan were talking to his partner.

He said: "Boy, you look like you need that three dollars. You look like you need some new boots, pants, and a new shirt. But maybe even more than that, you look like you need a nickel bar of lye soap and a good scrubbing down."

"The river's three miles off," responded Gitalong, "and I have no way of getting out there and back."

The stocky, thoughtful man kept staring. Ultimately, he said: "You listen to me, boy. There's nothing in this world a man can't do if he sets his heart to it. That includes you getting over to that river and taking a bath."

Suddenly, with a snap of his fingers, Al Grubb said: "I knew it. I knew it'd come to me. That bull-necked fellow is Tevis Blankenship."

From out in the road Bill Wentworth looked up. "Tevis? What in hell kind of a name is that?"

Grubb scowled. "Find that money and shut up." He turned and nodded at Marshal Nolan. "Tevis Blankenship. I met him once in Abilene. He's a drover from way back, Fred. Got a reputation from here to Salt Lake City."

"You didn't have to tell me he had a reputation," the marshal retorted drily. "I could tell that by looking at him. Tevis Blankenship, eh? Well, I'll remember that name. What else can you tell me about him, Al?"

Grubb scowled darkly. "Don't rightly recollect all the tales I heard, but it seems to me folks were sayin' around the Kansas plains the reason Tevis could bring herds through the Comanche country when no one else could, was because he went out of his way to hire the meanest, toughest riders he could find."

Nolan looked down his nose at Grubb. "That doesn't come exactly as any surprise, either," he murmured, and turned to Con Wheeler. "All right, I reckon you and your brother can head for your bedrolls. But there'll be an inquest when the circuit judge gets to Deadwood again, so I expect you'd better hang around until them."

Wheeler lost his smile. "When'll that be?" he asked.

Marshal Nolan shrugged and said: "Week. Maybe a little more than a week. He makes it here at least once a month and he was here no more than three weeks past."

Con Wheeler turned, caught his brother's attention, and those two exchanged a look which did not escape Marshal Nolan nor Al Grubb. When Con turned back, there was no hint in his facial expression as to what, exactly, that look might have meant.

"We'll be at the boarding house," he said.

Just then, up at the Bluebell Saloon, a fight broke out. Even though the marshal and the two deputies, out in the dusty roadway, could not see

45

that far, the sounds were unmistakable. Nolan jerked his head and started off at a trot. Grubb and Wentworth went jogging along in his wake.

Gitalong would have departed, too, but Ez Wheeler detained him by saying: "Tell us, boy, how come you to stay in a place like this?"

Gitalong looked from one of those similar, stocky men to the other, and shrugged. "I've been here since I was past fifteen. I don't know any other place to go. But even if I did, I don't have any way to get there."

Ez Wheeler sucked on his cigarette, tilted his head to catch the sounds of breaking furniture coming from the Bluebell with the air of a man who could tell exactly how that titanic struggle was progressing from those sounds. He gently shook his head as he grinned slightly at Gitalong.

"I can't figure out yet whether you're bad luck to my brother and me, boy, or whether we're bad luck to you."

Then Con Wheeler strolled up, considered Gitalong with his steady smoke-colored eyes and said nothing. When the pair of them were that close it wasn't hard to see the similarity, not just in general physical build, but also in facial structure, in their even, almost austere features, but perhaps most of all in the grayness of their wintry eyes and the thinness of their long-lipped mouths. Speaking or silent, the Wheeler brothers gave an impression of coiled rattlesnakes, of sheathed violence.

Con Wheeler, who had killed the Texan, dug around in a trouser pocket, brought up some silver, selected three cartwheels, and handed them to Gitalong. As he did this he said: "Boy, go buy yourself a cake of soap, some new pants, new boots, and a new shirt. If it comes to more than that, hunt me up and I'll pay the difference." He pocketed the balance of that money, looking steadily at Gitalong, then said: "And after this . . . keep out of our way. Come on, Ez, let's hit the blankets."

"Hold it, Con, hold it," Ez said, making no move to depart. "Can't leave the kid just like that."

As his brother held up and waited, Ez turned to Gitalong. "Son, you got enough private troubles without borrowin' more. Hitch a ride on some freight wagon or stage tonight and get out of Deadwood. If you have to come back, why then, let things settle for a week first. By then those big-mouthed Texans will be gone. Now, boy, you mark my word . . . those Texas boys want your scalp."

"They want yours, too," Gitalong replied.

Ez Wheeler made a frosty smile. "Yes, boy, they surely do. The difference is, though, they aren't goin' to lift our hair by a country mile, but they damned well *can* get yours. Now you just take my advice, boy."

Gitalong watched those two stocky men walk away, side by side, thinking that this was the second time the same day he'd got the same advice. He decided it was good advice and that he just might take it because now he had another three dollars. Abruptly recalling the other three dollars which had been struck from his outstretched hand by that bull-necked Texan named Blankenship, he crab-walked out into the roadway and began a systematic search of the powdery dust. Whether that money was his or not, it certainly belonged to somebody and didn't belong out there in the dirt.

It was a long and tiresome search but with such an incentive ahead, Gitalong persevered. He was still at it long after midnight, encouraged by discovering one of the cartwheels, and the possession of four dollars, more than he'd ever had before in his eighteen years of living. He kept after the remaining two dollars. With six dollars he could buy enough tinned goods to perhaps get him through the winter. He could even buy a horse, but he abandoned this notion at once because he had no way to care for a horse. Besides, in wintertime, hay cost money.

Several men riding southward out of Deadwood turned in their saddles to gaze with interest over where Gitalong was scuttling back and forth. Other men passed along the plank walks, and they too glanced over, the sober ones—a small minority—having no trouble at all in surmising what Gitalong was up to, the unsteady ones equally as positive that Gitalong was drunk as a coot.

Most of Deadwood's lights were out now. In the saloons and even in that hutment café, there were still lights—would in fact be lights until daylight returned—but generally, the town was quieting down a little. No matter how rugged men were, they were still in need of reinvigorating rest.

Jeremiah Perkins, with slack time on his hands every night about this time, sauntered down to help Gitalong look for the remaining two dollars. He pumped Gitalong dry about that earlier unpleasantness. Even after he'd extracted every detail, Jeremiah still kept worrying the topic like a pup worrying a bone. Neither he nor Gitalong saw the two approaching shadows—one tall the other not so tall but much broader—moving slowly southward from the vicinity of Ace Morton's saloon.

"Hey, you know what I think," Perkins said. "Those two Wheeler fellows are some kind of special agents . . . something like that."

Gitalong looked up, his gaze puzzled. "Why do you say that?" he asked. "What would special agents be around here for?"

Jeremiah snorted. "Hell. Deadwood's got more outlaws in it than any town you'll ever be in, Gitalong. I was readin' in a book a fellow left behind at the barn about these here secret operatives . . . they call 'em . . . who trail desperadoes to the ends of the earth."

Gitalong scuffed up a toe full of dust. The dying overhead light struck brightly against something round and shiny. He made a little triumphant grunt, stooped, and picked up another of the lost cartwheels, then he said: "Marshal Nolan would know if there were any desperadoes in Deadwood, Jeremiah. He wouldn't need any . . ."

"Aw," interrupted Jeremiah with a disdaining grunt, "Marshal Nolan . . ." Jeremiah caught sight of two quiet silhouettes over upon the plank walk and let his remonstrance die out. Those two watchers over there were Al Grubb and tall Bill Wentworth. Jeremiah was unsure how long they'd been there, how much they'd heard, or for that matter in his red-necked confusion he wasn't even certain how much he'd said, so he started legging it back up toward the livery barn. As he passed Gitalong, he muttered: "See you another time."

Bill Wentworth smiled. Even dour, beetle-browed Al Grubb was amused by Jeremiah's hasty departure. They knew about what Perkins had been on the verge of saying. It didn't antagonize them. They heard the same words every day almost, from some disgruntled man or woman.

"How many you found?" Bill Wentworth called out to Gitalong.

"All but one."

Wentworth wagged his head. "That's better than I did, but you'd be better to wait for sunup now."

Gitalong didn't answer.

The two lawmen, apparently on their way southward to the jailhouse for their after-midnight coffee break, stood watching a moment longer.

Al Grubb finally said: "Boy, want a little advice?"

Gitalong stopped scuffing, twisted, and gazed across the little intervening distance. "Can I guess first what it's going to be?"

Grubb shrugged, stared from beneath his black brows and waited.

"You're going to say I ought to leave town for a while . . . until that herd moves on northward."

Grubb solemnly inclined his head. "Maybe you know Texans and maybe you don't," he retorted. "But I do. They won't forget what happened in Deadwood tonight, and, Gitalong, you were the cause of it. Sure, that fellow Ezekiel Wheeler killed their friend, but you were the cause of it. They'll be after the pair of you. So, if I was you, I'd take a dollar or two of that money you got, buy a stage passage in any direction, and keep out of town for at least a week."

Gitalong stood out there, listening and looking. He knew Al Grubb. That is, he knew him by sight and they'd exchanged nods now and then. Grubb was a man who'd wade into his weight in wildcats. Men respected him. Upon occasion, they also feared him, which was the way it usually was with good peace officers.

"I reckon you're right," Gitalong conceded.

Bill Wentworth suddenly threw out a pointing arm. "Hey, Gitalong, look right there in front of you . . . there's the other one."

Swiftly, Gitalong glanced down, saw the partially disclosed roundness of a silver dollar, swooped it up, and straightened, happily smiling.

"Six dollars," he said. "I never had that much money before."

"Use it to keep alive," growled Al Grubb, then he turned and started on along toward the jailhouse. Bill Wentworth turned to follow along after him.

Gitalong went down between two sheds into the back alley and threaded his limping way through and around and over the refuse back there. He got to his shack, dropped down to crawl inside. After he thought about the day's events for some time in the dark, he took down a dented tin box in which he kept all the candle stubs he'd made a habit of watching for on his gleaning trips, lighted one, waited until its weak glow brightened into a steady pewter light, then he dredged up those six silver dollars from his ragged clothes, put them upon the packed earth in a shiny row, and rapturously gazed upon them.

He had never in his life seen such a wonderful sight.

But he had been through a lot this day, this night, so he dug in the old parfleche bag for a bone-dry splinter of jerky and leaned back upon the old pieces of rotting canvas and sacking which was his bed to dull the pangs of hunger while he watched the way the candlelight struck softly upon the row of silver dollars.

He would, he thought, do as Al Grubb and the others had said. He'd buy a seat on the morning coach and go somewhere for a week. This thought, too, was a heady one. He'd watched the coaches come and go for two years, had even occasionally dreamed of being on one, but had never before been even remotely likely to take such a thrilling ride. Now he would. There were other mining camps throughout the Black Hills. He knew them all by name without ever having seen any of them. There was one called Dog Town. That's where he'd go . . . Dog Town.

CHAPTER FIVE

Fred Nolan had his breakfast early, which was his custom, and afterward he ambled back down to the jailhouse to put the coffee pot on for Al and Bill. They usually had a cup or two while waiting for Deadwood to come to life, which it did early, but not seriously, because the night life sapped men.

He was just turning into his office when he heard the driver of the morning coach pop his whip and whoop at his six-up. Out of habit Fred paused, turned, and watched the horses hit their collars, yank the tugs taut in a singing lunge, drag the top-heavy old battered coach forward on its thorough-brace springs, and settle it back again with the usual head-snapping forward plunge. One thing about professional stage drivers, they made up for all the dreary monotony beyond and between the towns, by a flourish and a yell as they headed for the open country.

Fred smiled to himself. He'd been a driver once, down in Arizona where sometimes it got pretty hot between villages, between road agents and bandy-legged Apaches. The coach swayed and lurched as it headed straight toward him on its way out of town. Sometimes things got pretty interesting up here in the Black Hills country, too, what with professional outlaws and amateur road agents, usually starved-out gold seekers, making forays.

The driver saw Marshal Nolan in his doorway, saluted with his silver-ferruled coachman's long whip, popped the thing a foot over the backs of his horses, and set a booted foot lightly upon the brake handle to slow a trifle as he made a wide approach to the intersecting roadway. The shotgun guard casually nodded his head at the marshal. Fred waved back. One of the passengers, his head and one arm out a side window, also waved. Marshal Nolan included this man too in his wave.

He didn't recognize Gitalong until the coach was on past and cutting wide for the corner. Fred lowered his arm, turned to watch the coach make its wide swing, scuffing up billows of pungent dust, and lunge on around out of sight.

He went on inside, stoked up the little fire, put on the graniteware coffee pot, went to his desk. He was removing his hat when Al Grubb walked in accompanied by long-legged Bill Wentworth.

"You fellows know the crippled kid was on the morning coach?" Nolan asked.

Wentworth nodded downward at Grubb. "Al told him to git out of town for a few days . . . until those Texans pull out. Fred, that damned kid was out in the roadway last night about two o'clock siftin' the dust for those three cartwheels."

Grubb went over, lifted the coffee pot's lid, peered in, lowered the lid as he let out a yawn. "One of these nights," he disinterestedly said, "I'm goin' to get to bed before one o'clock."

"You wouldn't be able to sleep," stated Nolan. "You're out of the habit of hittin' the hay early. Say, kind of a busy evening last night so I never got much chance to tell you boys, but while I was havin' supper that young fellow the stage company sent here to manage their Deadwood office came over and sat with me."

"Neighborly," grunted Grubb, bending to peer into the stove's little firebox. "We got to empty the ashes one of these days. There's not enough draught getting through."

"There's a bullion coach coming through," Nolan went on.

Bill Wentworth, in the act of rolling a cigarette, lifted his eyes. Over at the little stove Al Grubb swung his head. Neither of them spoke.

Marshal Nolan smiled without any show of mirth or amusement.

"Nice," he said. "I thought you boys would be pleased."

Wentworth resumed his work.

Grubb straightened up, turned his back on the stove, and said: "What are the details?"

"All he told me was that there was one coming through Deadwood with dust and nuggets from the outlying camps," Nolan told them. "He didn't know when, but he said he'd find out today and let me know."

"And who else will he let know?" Al growled. "Are we supposed to meet it out somewhere and ride escort for it through our territory?"

Nolan nodded. "That's the custom, Al. We've done it before. As for the stage company manager spillin' the beans . . . he doesn't have to and if you'd think a minute you'd know that. Any time a bullion coach starts going through the diggings picking up gold, folks see it, know what's going on. It doesn't take much intelligence or even very good eyesight for men to understand what's happening. Every miner who consigns gold has a mouth."

"Usually a big mouth," muttered Wentworth, lighting up. "It'd sure please me if the danged Army would take over this escort detail. Seems to be more a soldier's work than a civilian lawman's work. Besides, Fred, this hasn't been too good a year in the diggings. There's more cussed lawlessness going on in the hills now than . . ."

"All we've got to do," broke in Nolan, "is round us up ten or twelve buckaroos like we've done before, pick up the coach eight or ten miles out, and ride with it eight or ten miles southward. After that, it's up to the next lawmen. Sure it's been a poor year, Bill, but hungry miners aren't going to risk attacking fifteen or twenty armed men."

Al Grubb turned to consider the singing coffee pot. "Come and get it," he said. As he reached for one of the three tin cups suspended from nails behind the stovepipe, he said: "Fred, except for that kid with the bent leg and those two Wheelers, we'd have a natural-formed posse in that Texas drover crew. Say what you like about Texans, but when I'm in trouble and need someone to protect my back, I'll take Texas boys any day in the week."

Bill Wentworth was strolling on across to get his cup of coffee as he said: "You sure didn't act like you had any love for Texas drovers last night when you grabbed that Blankenship fellow by the gullet." Bill leaned far over to take down his cup. "I can just see that fellow helpin' us out now, too."

Just then the roadside door opened. A gray-headed, big, stoop-shouldered man entered, nodded at the three, and hesitated as though he thought he might be interrupting something.

Marshal Nolan, in the act of reaching for his cup, said: " 'Morning, Elisha. That saddle I told you about yesterday is out in the horse shed behind the jailhouse. The rigging's not busted yet but it's sure suffering from a bad case of sweat rot."

The saddle and harness maker nodded. "I'll have it for you no later than day after tomorrow, Marshal."

"Care for a cup of java?" Nolan asked, holding out his own cup.

The big man shook his head. "Finished breakfast not more than twenty minutes ago, Marshal," he said. "But thanks for the offer. There's something you could tell me if you would."

"Sure, Elisha. What's on your mind?"

"That crippled kid . . . the one they call Gitalong . . . he came rushin' into the shop last night and wanted Delia to keep three silver dollars for him."

"What about it?"

"I wouldn't let her, Marshal. I told him to get out of the shop. Delia's madder than a hornet at me. I said he more than likely stole that money and she says he didn't ever. . . ."

"He didn't steal it, Elisha," Nolan interrupted. "But last night you no doubt heard that a man got killed in a gunfight. Well, Gitalong and his three dollars were involved."

The harness maker looked astounded. "You mean to tell me that ragged, starved cripple shot someone?"

"No, no. Not what I'm saying. Gitalong didn't do the shooting. A man named Ezekiel Wheeler did that. But it was over Gitalong and his three dollars." When Nolan saw the puzzlement deepening in Elisha Wilson's face, he added: "Don't worry about it. It doesn't concern you anyway. But Gitalong didn't steal that three dollars, so I reckon your daughter was right."

"Still," persisted the big, stooped man bleakly, "I don't like him hanging around the shop. I don't like Delia feeling sorry for him."

Bill Wentworth, silent up till now, turned and gazed at the saddle maker through an exhaled grayish cloud of fragrant smoke. "I got a feelin' that kid doesn't enjoy bein' hungry all the time, Mister Wilson," he said coldly. "And I also got a hunch he doesn't enjoy goin' scuttlin' around in rags on his crooked leg. I reckon you're entitled to your opinion about Gitalong, though . . . same as me or anyone." Wentworth turned his back on Wilson and sipped his coffee.

Without a word, the saddle maker departed.

For a little while the three sipped their coffee in silence.

But they weren't concerned with Gitalong. They'd pushed him out of their minds the moment Wilson's interlude ended with the harness maker's leave-taking. What they were privately considering again was that bullion coach. There was no surer way under the sun to get killed than by escorting a stage with a fortune in raw gold on board, and despite all their reassuring talk to one another, this was uppermost in all their minds.

Even when they didn't seem to be thinking about it—as when black-eyed, cruel-mouthed Ace Morton walked in and slammed the door, gazing sardonically across the room.

The owner of the Bluebell Saloon said: "The rest of us got to work in this town while you boys got plenty of time for a little visitin' with coffee."

Morton was a solid two-hundred pounder balanced upon the legs of a fighter. He was brutal and seemed entirely without feelings, but he ran honest games at his saloon and gave full measure over the bar. He had one trait though that had never endeared him to anyone—he was sarcastic. More than that, Ace Morton was viciously sarcastic. He held people in contempt. Sometimes he even seemed to hold himself along with everyone else, in contempt. His sarcasm was cutting or slashing, depending upon his mood, but it was never less than stinging, as now, when Fred Nolan and his deputies turned to gaze over at Morton.

Al Grubb growled: "What got you out of bed before noon . . . someone buy a saddle bum a drink at the Bluebell and you want to file a complaint?"

Morton's black stare settled upon Grubb. These two, built the same and in other ways not too dissimilar, had been like flint on steel since their first meeting, but Morton let Grubb's remark go by.

"Marshal, whenever you finish your coffee, maybe you can find time to stroll on up to Doc Wolfert's place. There's been a little accident and a miner came in a while back to tell me about it."

"An accident?" demanded Bill Wentworth. "Why should anyone tell you, of all people, Morton? You're nothin' but a saloonkeeper in Deadwood, that's all."

Morton's black gaze brightened perceptibly. "Just a saloonkeeper," he said to Wentworth. "But you know something, Deputy. I can buy and sell ten like you out of my watch pocket any day in the year."

"The accident," stated Fred Nolan, putting aside his cup and starting across the room. "What were you told about it, Morton?"

"Go see for yourself, Nolan. Doc Wolfert's expecting you," replied Morton, and walked back out of the office.

Nolan jerked his head. Grubb and Wentworth put aside their java mugs. The three of them left the jailhouse northward bound. As they moved past the stage office a distraught young man intercepted them.

"You heard about the accident," he said, making a troubled statement of this remark. "I can't imagine how it happened."

Marshal Nolan, looking straight at the man, said: "What about it? Where did it happen? What are the details? All we know is what Ace Morton just told us."

"The horses piled up, Marshal, about four miles beyond town. They were evidently traveling at a fast gait and one of them stumbled, or fell . . .

something like that . . . and the whole outfit piled up. I'm waiting for the driver and guard to get here. Some miners are fetching them in a wagon."

"Hurt?" asked Bill Wentworth.

The stage office manager nodded. "Broken arms and ribs, they say, Deputy, although all any of us have to go on so far is . . ."

"Wait a minute," broke in Al Grubb in his growling tone. "There was a passenger aboard, wasn't there?"

Fred Nolan turned on Grubb. "Come on. I think the answer to your question is up at Wolfert's house."

They hastened along until, in front of a rough-board house, squarely built and functionally ugly, Nolan stopped and turned.

"Al, get your horse, ride out and have a look at the wreckage. If there are any busted-legged horses, shoot 'em. Make sure you take a good look around."

Grubb nodded, turned, and walked away southward, back the way he had just come. Nolan and Wentworth went on up to the front door of that slab house, knocked, and were admitted by a bushy-headed, lean man who looked to be in his early fifties.

"Ace Morton said you had someone up here we might be interested in seeing," said Marshal Nolan. "Who is it, Doc?"

Wolfert was a gloomy-looking quiet man. No

one knew exactly why a practicing physician and surgeon would lose himself in a place like Deadwood, Dakota Territory, but no one asked, either. There were not very many men in the diggings who could have, or who would have, given straightforward answers to that question, and it was therefore never asked.

Doc Wolfert gravely nodded, turned without a word, and led Nolan and Wentworth into an adjoining room. He halted in the doorway to say: "Some Indians brought him in on a travois. The ride didn't help him much."

"Who's him?" asked Marshal Nolan, shouldering past. He went across to the bed, halted, and looked down at the emaciated, gray, and bloody face.

"Gitalong!"

Bill Wentworth also came over and stood gazing at the battered eighteen-year-old. When Doc Wolfert came up, Wentworth said softly: "Looks like the world fell on him, Doc. How bad is it?"

"Bad, gentlemen," Wolfert quietly stated. "As I understood it from the Indians, the coach turned completely over with him inside. The driver and guard were thrown clear, but this one . . . he was still inside when the Indians rode down and got him out." Wolfert leaned slightly and with an impersonal, professional look upon the unconscious, thin victim of the accident, he said:

"I undressed him to put him to bed and to also clean and bandage him. Have either of you ever seen this lad stripped? No? Well, he's as near to being pure skin and bones as a person can be, and still walk around." Wolfert straightened back up. "And that leg. It's been broken badly sometime and allowed to mend without splints or anything else. Fortunately though, it was broken again in the same place when the coach turned over with him."

"Fortunately?" Fred Nolan repeated, looking around.

Wolfert nodded. "I re-set it, gentlemen, the way it should originally have been set. He may have a slight limp . . . if he lives to recover . . . but that's all he'll have. I think even that may disappear in time. Still, it'll be a long, long time before this boy walks again, if he ever does. He's also got two cracked ribs, a dislocated jaw, and . . ."

"Was he conscious when the Indians brought him, Doc?" Bill Wentworth broke in to ask.

Wolfert shook his head. "Hardly. In fact, at first glance I thought he was dead. I was about to tell the Indians to take him down to you at the jailhouse when he whimpered." Wolfert paused, looked down then up again, and murmured: "This is going to be expensive, gentlemen. All he had on him was four silver dollars. I'm a humanitarian, but even humanitarians need money for bandaging and medicines. Who'll pay for what I've already done and . . . if he lives . . . what else has to be done?"

Neither Nolan nor Wentworth answered. They didn't know who would pay.

CHAPTER SIX

Someone entered Doc Wolfert's outer room and slammed the door. The doctor excused himself to go see who this was, and meanwhile Fred Nolan and Bill Wentworth exchanged a look.

"One thing with doctors," Bill said drily. "They've always got one uppermost thought . . . who's going to pay."

Nolan had no comment to make about this. All he said was: "What is it about some folks, Bill, that makes them just naturally unlucky? All this kid was doing was trying to get out of town for a few days. That damned coach has been making the same run for five years . . . but this time, when Gitalong's aboard, it's got to pile up and hurt people."

The door behind them opened and Doc Wolfert stood aside as two men entered. Without speaking these two nodded, walked up, and gazed down at Gitalong, scarcely breathing, battered and bloody. One of the men groped for a chair and sat down.

Marshal Nolan, looking at this one, said: "Mister Wheeler, you don't look so good."

"Don't feel so good," conceded the stocky man, looking from Gitalong to Fred Nolan. "Something I ate, Marshal." The gray, steady eyes brightened with an ironic amusement. "I've always heard Deadwood was a dangerous place, but I had no idea that included the food."

Bill Wentworth sympathetically inclined his head. "I've had the same thing a time or two, Mister Wheeler."

"What do you do for it?" asked the pale man, switching his attention from Nolan to Wentworth.

"Drink milk for three, four days is all. Doc here calls it some kind of poisoning."

"Ptomaine," the doctor stated, looking up from a bandage he was folding and refolding. "If you'll come with me, I'll get you some powders."

The other Wheeler said: "Wait a minute, Doc. This crippled kid . . . was he in that coach that piled up this morning?"

When Wolfert answered in the affirmative, the Wheeler brothers exchanged a long glance.

Con, the ill one, shook his head. Ez pursed his lips. "Marshal," the latter murmured, "I'm not a superstitious man . . . but by glory every time we turn around . . . here's this crippled kid again."

Getting ready to leave the room, Nolan commented: "Coincidence."

Bill Wentworth followed Nolan, but Bill was still thinking about what Doc Wolfert had said before he'd left the room to admit the Wheelers.

"About who'll pay, Doc . . . I got no idea. How far will the kid's four dollars go?"

"I've already used up more than that much

in splints, bandages, liniments, and my time, Deputy."

Con Wheeler's gray face lifted, his wintry gaze passed from one face to the other. "You mean to tell me," he growled, "you fellows aren't goin' to be able to see your way clear to patch this kid up?"

Nolan shook his head. "No, that's not it, Mister Wheeler. Gitalong will be cared for. What we're puzzling over is who, afterward, is going to pay his bill with Doc Wolfert."

Ez Wheeler, still there at bedside, turned and looked his bitter scorn at the two lawmen and the medical practitioner. "If it was a horse, you'd just shoot it. Why don't you simplify things and give the kid the same dose?"

Doc Wolfert was embarrassed, but Fred Nolan wasn't; he was piqued.

Before either he or Bill Wentworth could speak up, Con Wheeler, sitting over on a chair staring at the injured lad, said: "How much will it total up to, Doc?"

Wolfert shrugged, gazing at Gitalong's outline in the bed. "It depends. If he died before nightfall . . . nothing. His four dollars will take care of it."

"Dies?" Con Wheeler said. "He's that bad off?"

"Yes. But mainly because of his emaciated, undernourished condition. I'd venture the statement that this boy hasn't had a decent hot meal in perhaps six months or a year."

"In this town," Con Wheeler said acidly, "that's not too unusual, I'd guess, Doc. What have you got for my ptomaine . . . or whatever I've got?"

"I'll go get you some powders that'll . . ."

"Wait a minute. First things first. About the boy . . . how much, Doctor?"

"Guessing, Mister Wheeler, I'd say perhaps thirty, forty dollars."

Con looked up at Ezekiel. Fred and Bill Wentworth noticed that same odd look pass between them they'd noticed the night before right after the killing of the Texas drover.

Ez said: "We'll stand good for it, Doc. Now, go fetch Con those powders for his stomach ache."

Wolfert left the room. Fred Nolan stood awkwardly looking like he wanted to say something but didn't know how to say it. Bill Wentworth, too, seemed abashed, but Bill finally got a rough sentence out.

"I'll kick in ten of that forty," he said.

Neither Con nor Ez acted as though they'd heard Bill. They gazed toward the bed with the gloom of the shaded room engulfing them until Doc Wolfert came back, then Con got up, paid for the powders he received, nodded all around, and followed his brother out of the room.

Doc Wolfert listened for his roadside outer door to close, then he lifted his shoulders and dropped them resignedly. "By tomorrow those two will be fifty miles away from here," he pessimistically declared.

Fred Nolan didn't think so. Neither did Bill Wentworth, but they didn't disagree; they simply walked out of the room, out of Wolfert's combination residence and clinic. They halted out in the dazzling morning brightness with the noises and smells of Deadwood piling up around them. They were better judges of men than Doc Wolfert was, at least in their private opinions they thought they were.

On the way southward toward the jailhouse they were brought sharply around by some rearward calls and yells. A slow-moving old wagon was coming into town from the east. Clearly discernible in it were two men swaddled in blankets.

"The driver and guard," said Bill. "Maybe we ought to go back and be on hand when Doc patches them up."

"Later," said Nolan. "Here comes Al."

They went on down and waited in front of the jailhouse until Grubb rode up, stepped down, looped his reins, and nodded solemnly. The three passed on inside where Grubb removed his hat, swiped at sweat upon his forehead, and looked over at the pained face of the marshal.

"You want to know what happened out there?" Grubb said. "You're not goin' to believe me, Fred. What Morton said was right . . . but not altogether right. A lead horse did go down and the other horses did whip up over on top of him causin' the coach to break up. But that lead horse didn't just step in a dog hole or get tangled up and fall . . . he was shot."

Nolan and Wentworth digested this slowly. Al Grubb went across to the water bucket with a dipper in it, took a long drink, quietly belched, and faced back around, his gaze saturnine.

"Go on," said Marshal Nolan. "Let's have all of it."

Grubb shook his head. "That *is* all of it. Maybe it was those Indians who brought Gitalong in. Maybe they were out huntin' and a stray shot felled the lead critter. Anyway, he had a carbine hole in his head about an inch below the left ear. He never knew what hit him. He must've fallen like stone and the whole works piled up on top of him. By the time I got out there some miners from a nearby drift had cut loose the other horses, had shot one with two busted legs, while some other miners had already started for town with the whip and the armed guard."

"Anyone say they heard the shot?" asked Wentworth.

Grubb nodded. "Couple of miners said they heard a shot, but none of 'em saw anyone with a rifle, except those cussed Indians, and there's just one thing wrong with that. The Indians were atop a little hill. Even the miners all swore to that. But the bullet that killed that horse struck him straight on, not from any downward-anglin' position."

"One of the miners, then," suggested Marshal Nolan.

Al shrugged and turned back for another long drink of cold water. As he wiped his mouth, Bill Wentworth's eyes narrowed slightly.

"All right," he said. "Out with it, Al . . . what's on your mind?"

"The Texans," Grubb stated quietly and hesitantly.

Marshal Nolan frowned faintly. "Kill a good horse, upset a six-up hitch and a coach, injure a driver and an armed guard . . . just to get even with a crippled kid? Seems pretty drastic to me, Al."

Grubb was unperturbed. "Yeah, and it seemed the same way to me all the way back to town, Fred. But last night Blankenship made his threat against the kid, and today the kid's all busted up in a stagecoach wreck."

"Coincidence," said the marshal as he went across to his desk and sat down.

Grubb still persisted in the same unperturbed manner. "Probably, Fred. Probably coincidence, only it sticks in my craw that someone shot that lead horse when the outfit was traveling at breakneck speed. That someone . . . whoever he was . . . knew damned well what would happen. Now, he wasn't one of those scruffy Indians, because none of them were down low enough to have fired that shot. It wasn't a miner . . . at least all the miners say it couldn't have been, or they'd have seen the shooter. Now you tell me then, who does that leave . . . barrin' armed angels wingin' their way through the countryside?"

"The Texans," confirmed Bill Wentworth. "And, Fred . . . don't forget they had a man killed last night. They had plenty of reason."

"But Gitalong didn't kill that cowboy," protested the marshal. "If they were going after anyone, they would've gone after Ez Wheeler."

Al Grubb said drily: "The day's not over yet." He held out his hand to Wentworth for Bill's tobacco and papers.

"How did they know Gitalong would be on that stage?" Fred asked, swinging around in his chair.

"That'd be no problem," Grubb retorted. "They could see the idiot lookin' out a window . . . or maybe they had a fellow or two idlin' around town this morning who saw him get aboard."

But Marshal Nolan still wasn't convinced. He, like just about everyone else in the country, viewed Gitalong as someone totally unimportant, someone seen and recognized and passed over. That the Texans were violent men capable of such a thing he didn't deny, but it seemed far-fetched to believe they'd risk their lives to murder a crippled scarecrow who hadn't really hurt them in any way.

Al Grubb lit up, went over to the door, and reached for the latch. "Got to put up my horse," he said, and stepped outside. But he wasn't gone more than a half minute before he opened the door and looked in.

"Fred, better come have a look," he said. "Blankenship and his gun-savvy crew are back in town."

Immediately Nolan and Wentworth crossed to the jailhouse door, stepped through to join Grubb on the plank walk, and gazed northward where, through the dust and noise and movement of Deadwood's customary traffic, they had an excellent view of six mounted men riding down into town in a bunched-up group, armed with Winchesters and sidearms, seeming not even to be talking among themselves as they walked their mounts along. The one out in front was unmistakably bull-necked Tevis Blankenship.

Wentworth muttered audibly: "If my name was Wheeler about now, I reckon I'd scuttle around in search of a hole to creep into."

Nolan said: "Go on, Al, put your horse away, and afterward, stay around up there near the livery barn. Bill, you go on up to Morton's place and see what they say at the bar. Me, I'm curious about whether that driver or guard saw the rifleman who downed their lead horse. If they did, I want 'em to walk on over to Ace's place and have a drink with me."

Grubb went out, untied his animal, and went walking northward, leading the beast. Wentworth cut straight across the roadway, reached the far walkway, and also headed north. Fred Nolan stood down there in front of his jailhouse carefully eyeing those six Texans as they came along as far as Morton's saloon before turning in, alighting at the hitch rack, and lining up over there.

Fred saw Blankenship gaze across at the hutment café where his cowboy had died in a roar of gunfire the night before. He saw how Blankenship looked farther southward, down where Fred was standing, and although the distance was too great for the marshal to study Blankenship's expression, he had an intuitive feeling that Blankenship was smiling exultantly.

The Texans ambled over and stepped up onto the plank walk, elbowed through the sidewalk traffic, and disappeared inside the Bluebell. When the last one faded from sight Marshal Nolan struck out for Doc Wolfert's place to get some answers, if he could.

CHAPTER SEVEN

The first in a series of disappointments met Marshal Nolan up at the doctor's establishment. Neither the armed guard nor the whip had any idea about how their accident had happened. The guard had a broken right arm.

He complained bitterly: "Just what a shotgun guard needs . . . a lousy busted arm. I'll be down to eatin' my moccasins before this thing heals and I can get another job."

The driver could only shrug. "One minute we was sailin' along, the next minute . . . *whoosh!* I'm goin' through the air like a bird. Reckon one of the lead critters stepped in a dog hole or got fouled in his harness or something."

Fred told neither of them what had caused that lead horse to fall. He did ask if they remembered seeing anyone alongside the road anywhere, perhaps a hunter with a carbine, maybe a miner or a cowboy out pot hunting.

Neither of them recollected seeing anyone like that although the whip said: "There was a little band of Indians atop a knoll watchin' us go past. I remember them because I recall how sorry and scruffy they looked. Made me think how different Injuns used to be when I first come to the Black

Hills . . . big, proud devils in them days." He shook his head.

Nolan left the two having gained no additional information, and walked back outside.

Doc Wolfert followed him out the door, glanced back to make sure neither of the stage men had followed, and said quietly: "Gitalong regained consciousness a while back."

Nolan looked around at Wolfert, immediately wondering what Gitalong might remember and be able to tell him. Wolfert must have guessed how Nolan's thoughts were running. As he reached behind himself for the latch string he said: "Give him until morning, Marshal, then you can talk to him."

"Yeah, I can do that," said Nolan. "What're his chances now, Doc?"

Wolfert wouldn't commit himself. He simply shrugged and disappeared back into the house.

Across the road and southward, at the Bluebell Saloon, Bill Wentworth walked out onto the plank walk and looked up and down the roadway. When he saw Marshal Nolan up in front of Wolfert's, he faintly lifted his shoulders. The marshal interpreted this to mean Bill had learned nothing inside. He stepped down into the roadway and walked over where Wentworth stood.

Bill gently waggled his head and said in a low tone: "Nothing. They're just drinkin' and belly-achin' about the distance they still got to go with their herd."

Fred looked over toward the livery barn. Al was smoking in the doorway and idly conversing with Jeremiah Perkins. He looked back at the batwing, louvred doors behind him. With Wentworth trailing, he went inside.

The Bluebell didn't have very many patrons. It was still a mite early in the day for serious drinking. There was a nest of card players over in a shadowy corner and along Morton's bar there were the six Texans and three or four others. Perhaps in all there were fourteen or fifteen men inside.

Marshal Nolan sauntered up and settled in beside Tevis Blankenship, hooked his elbows upon the counter, and gave Ace Morton stare for stare. He said: "Couple of ales, Ace." Recalling Morton's sarcasm down at the jailhouse, Nolan said: "Good to see you working for a change. Too much loafing will make your bile doggish."

Morton's black eyes flashed but he continued to get the ale without comment.

Bill Wentworth, on Nolan's far side, chuckled to himself. On Nolan's left side, Tevis Blankenship looked stonily straight ahead into the back-bar mirror until Marshal Nolan addressed him.

"I'm sorry about that man of yours, last night," Fred said. "But you'll have to admit he was pushin' a little hard when he got shot."

Blankenship acted initially as though he hadn't heard. Then he lifted his empty glass, swirled it, and minutely examined it through narrowed eyes. Finally, he slowly nodded and said: "You could be right, Marshal. It goes against the grain because Reb was a good man, but you could be right."

Nolan said nothing more until Morton brought his drink, and Wentworth's drink, set them down with unnecessary hardness, and scooped up Fred's coin and walked away but not before glaring at Nolan for several seconds.

"Still and all," Blankenship said, not moving to look around. "You're goin' to have that inquest, aren't you, Marshal?"

Fred was hoisting his ale glass as he said: "Yes. That's the law. We always have inquests after killings."

Blankenship signaled Ace for a refill. Down the bar to his left were his men, laughing and noisily talking now, either indifferent to the law's presence among them or unaware of it.

When Morton placed his refill in front of him, Blankenship said: "Marshal, what happened on the road this morning? We heard there was a pile-up or some kind of an accident."

"Coach upended," Nolan told him. "Lead horse tripped and fell."

"Anyone hurt?"

"Three. The whip and guard, and that crippled kid."

Blankenship tossed off his drink, leaned forward, and set the glass down precisely in its little wet circle.

"Hurt bad, Marshal, any of those fellows?" he inquired.

"They'll make it . . . with luck. The crippled kid was worst off. Doc says it's touch and go with him."

"Too bad," Blankenship said in a mumble.

Nolan had nothing to say, but when the Texan turned his head and glanced upward, Nolan didn't look like he believed Blankenship's expression of sympathy.

The Texan shrugged. "Well, let me put it another way then," he said, looking straight at Marshal Nolan. "I'm sorry the kid got hurt in anythin' as silly as a busted stagecoach. I got no reason to love him, nor them two that killed Reb, either, and I'll be honest enough to tell you that straight out, Marshal."

"You figure to light out pretty soon now?" Fred asked.

Blankenship inclined his head, turned back to studying that empty shot glass in its sticky pool, and said: "Pretty quick now, Marshal, pretty quick." He paused, pushed the little glass away, looked to the left along the bar where his men were drinking and noisily talking, swung back as he straightened up off the bar. He studied Nolan's face before saying: "Got a little unfinished business to tend to first though, Marshal . . . that black-browed deputy of yours who grabbed me last night when I was off guard. Sort of like to settle with him before I haul on out of here."

The marshal finished his ale, turned his back to the bar, and gazed around the room. Those poker players over in their gloomy corner were still at it. "Forget it," he growled at Blankenship. "It was one of those fifty-fifty things . . . you asked for it, on your part, and on Grubb's part, he was a little hair-triggered. It's over now and done with, so if that's all that's holding you back, why you can line out your herd come sunup and be halfway through the hills by tomorrow night."

Blankenship nodded impassively. "Reckon I could at that, Marshal. Reckon I could at that. Only trouble is . . . I don't aim to."

Ace Morton came down behind the marshal, leaned far over, and said: "Nolan, there's a fellow outside sent in word he wants to see you."

Fred twisted for a look at Morton. It struck him oddly that whoever was waiting outside to see him wouldn't walk right on into the saloon.

Morton, guessing what that raised-eyebrow look signified, shrugged and walked off.

Blankenship, who had heard, said banteringly: "Must be a man of the cloth, Marshal . . . him not wanting to come into a saloon. You got a pet preacher?"

Nolan and Wentworth left the saloon. The man they met out on the plank walk was Ez Wheeler.

In response to Nolan's faintly perplexed look, Wheeler said: "With the Texans inside I thought it might cause less trouble if I waited outside for you, Marshal."

Fred nodded. Wheeler was making sense so far. Over across the road Al Grubb was still loafing in the livery barn doorway. A big freight outfit, two wagons double-tongued with the full hitch of mules out in front ten teams long, creaked and groaned its way southward taking up almost half the broad roadway.

Ezekiel Wheeler held out his left hand to Marshal Nolan, opened the fingers, and exposed a flattened lead bullet on his palm.

"Souvenir," he said, speaking so softly it was difficult for Nolan to hear him over the racket of that passing freight train. "Take it, Marshal."

Fred took the slug, examined it closely, and raised quizzical eyes.

Wheeler's wintry stare was sardonic. "Those powders Doc Wolfert gave Con worked so well we decided we'd go for a little ride in the fresh morning air, Marshal. Nice riding weather."

The marshal dropped the flattened slug into a vest pocket. "You want to talk here or down at the jailhouse?" he asked.

Wheeler's look of cold amusement didn't alter. "Here'll be fine, Marshal. We dug that slug out of the head of the lead horse that caused the accident that busted up the crippled kid. Reckon it wasn't any accident after all."

Nolan looked over where Al was leaning. He looked around at Bill Wentworth. "Go tell Al what Blankenship said, then the pair of you get your dinner and meet me at the office in an hour or so."

Wentworth dutifully moved off.

Fred took Ez Wheeler's arm, turned, and started sauntering southward with him. "We knew about that horse being shot," he said as they paced along through the midday sidewalk traffic. "One of my deputies rode out earlier, Mister Wheeler."

"Good. That shows you boys aren't sleeping, Marshal. But tell me this . . . who shot the horse and why?"

"The why of it's pretty obvious, isn't it, Mister Wheeler? Someone wanted to pile up the coach. My deputies seem to think someone wanted to get back at the crippled kid over what happened because of him last night."

"That'd be the Texans, then," stated Wheeler. Then he added something that made Fred Nolan turn his head and gaze thoughtfully at the older man. "And they could be right, too, except for one thing, Marshal. Didn't your man notice that the trajectory of that bullet, and the distance ahead of the coach of that shot horse, which was at least forty feet, would have made it impossible for the bushwhacker to see who was inside the coach?"

Al hadn't said anything about that at all. In fact, as Fred strolled thoughtfully along with Ez Wheeler, it struck him that even if the bushwhacker had seen Gitalong get aboard that coach in town, as he and his men had discussed earlier at the jailhouse, he couldn't possibly have ridden so far in so short a length of time, right through the honeycombed placer diggings where miners were as thick as hair on a dog's back, without being seen.

"We discussed it a little," Nolan said, halting upon the plank walk's edge. Directly across the road was his jailhouse.

Wheeler clasped both hands behind his back. "I'll tell you what my brother and I think, Marshal, for what it's worth. We think that whoever downed that lead horse was already out there in hiding alongside the road somewhere."

"Possible," assented Fred, thinking the same thing but being cautious.

"We also figure he had a special reason for upending that coach." Wheeler's wintry gray glance met Nolan's gaze. "Care to hear some more speculation, Marshal?" he asked.

Fred nodded. From the corner of his eye he saw Blankenship and his Texas crew stroll out of the Bluebell and head for their horses at the hitch rail.

"Well, Marshal, it's all guesswork, but we think it's damned likely that someone shot that horse, piled up that coach, and hurt those men . . . not out of any vengeful feelings at all . . . but just to see how a coach would pile up when the lead horse was dumped in a full run."

Very gradually now, a conclusion fell into place in Fred Nolan's mind. He stared at Ez Wheeler. The older man was regarding him stonily.

"Go on," the marshal said. "There's more and I'd like to hear it."

"I reckon you would at that," Wheeler stated drily. "All right, Marshal. There's a bullion coach picking up fine gold throughout the diggings north and west of Deadwood. Directly now it'll be heading down this way. It'll have an escort as far as the limits of your territory, but after that it'll be your responsibility. You understand what I'm saying?"

Nolan understood perfectly. It chilled him to think that news of the coming of the bullion stage had preceded its actual arrival like this, that outlaws were already making plans and perfecting systems to halt it and plunder it.

"Pleasant prospect, isn't it?" said Ez Wheeler, watching Marshal Nolan's face. "Still, the forewarned are the forearmed. See you around town, Marshal." Wheeler stepped down into the dust and went hiking straight toward the yonder hutment café.

Fred went across to his jailhouse office to do a little thinking. Later, when Al and Bill ambled in, he told them what Ezekiel Wheeler had suggested. They were, at first anyway, nonplussed, even skeptical, but as time wore on they came more and more to act as though they accepted Wheeler's theory of the piled-up daytime coach.

Grubb said: "Fred, just where do these Wheeler boys fit in? All of a sudden here they are in Deadwood. They dress well, live at the boarding house, eat regular, but they never go out to the diggings or make any move to set up in business hereabouts."

Nolan pointed to a stack of Wanted posters. "You might try to get a line on them from those flyers, Al. Personally, if they're outlaws of some kind, my judgment's going bad on me."

"Special agents," suggested lanky Bill Wentworth. "If they aren't some kind of lawmen, how come they went out and dug that bullet out of the dead horse and why did they do all that figurin' on why the coach was piled up?"

Watching Al unenthusiastically approach the pile of Wanted posters, Nolan said: "I don't know. All I'm sure of, boys, is that if Ez Wheeler is right, we're heading into some real bad trouble the minute that damned bullion coach gets into our territory."

"Those bullion coaches are always trouble," Al declared gruffly.

"But this could be a lot different, boys," Nolan said. "A lot different."

CHAPTER EIGHT

Marshal Nolan had his midday meal and returned to the jailhouse just in time to meet the stage company manager leaving the office. Before the stage-line man said a word Nolan knew the worst; it was indelibly stamped across the features of Bill Wentworth and Al Grubb, inside the office.

"All right," Nolan grumbled at the stage company employee. "When is it due?"

"Day after tomorrow, Marshal. I said I'd find out and let you know."

"I'm obliged," growled Nolan as he eased the stage manager out of his office and waited for Grubb or Wentworth to say something. Neither of them did.

The roadside door opened, Doc Wolfert walked in, looked around, closed the door behind himself, saying then: "Marshal, I think you'd better go and talk to the crippled lad."

Fred got up. So did Al and Bill. Wolfert opened the door, stepped back outside, and swung in beside Marshal Nolan as they headed north.

"He asked for you the minute I went back to change his dressings."

"Rational, Doc?"

"As rational as I am, Marshal."

"What's on his mind?"

"He didn't tell me. Only asked me to get you."

"How is he otherwise?"

"Well . . . I'm having hot meals sent in from the boarding house. He seems to be holding his own, but, Marshal, that jaw of his is badly swollen, so don't make him talk any more than is absolutely necessary."

As they turned in at the doctor's place, Nolan said: "I don't think I'll have to make him talk at all. I'm just here to listen."

Whether this enigmatic statement had any effect upon Wolfert or not wasn't immediately obvious. He opened the door and stood back while the trio of lawmen walked inside. Afterward, he lit a small coal-oil lamp, held it in front, and walked on into the room where Gitalong lay in sooty gloom. The blinds were all drawn. The air was stale and there was an unpleasant, gloomy atmosphere.

Al Grubb growled at Doc Wolfert: "You got some objection to fresh air? This room smells like a Pawnee sweat house."

The doctor moved to open a window, saying as he did so: "I didn't want roadway noises keeping him from resting."

Marshal Nolan crossed to the bed, saw Gitalong's opaque eyes open, swing, and settle upon his face. He smiled a little and Gitalong's cruelly unbalanced face with its badly bruised and swollen left jaw, made a feeble grin back.

"Marshal . . . I saw . . . just before the accident . . . I saw a rifle barrel up ahead in some rocks. Saw smoke come out of it, too. Then everything happened at once. . . . Then I woke up in here."

"Gitalong, how far ahead of the coach did you spot that gun barrel?"

"Maybe a hundred feet, maybe a little more than that. It was off to the left of the road. How I happened to see it . . . I was watching some Indians atop a little hill, and the sunlight struck that barrel makin' it all silvery. Then it went off."

"Who was holding it, Gitalong?"

"Didn't see him, Marshal. Only the barrel. Then . . ."

"Yeah. O.K., son, you just lie easy now and don't tell anyone else about this. You understand?"

Gitalong's head weakly moved on his pillow. He gazed at the three tough-looking law officers. "You goin' . . . back out there . . . Marshal?"

Nolan nodded. "We'll take that little ride, yes. You go on back to sleep now. If we find out anything, we'll let you know."

"Marshal, I had four dollars left. . . ."

Al Grubb said: "Never you mind about that. You've still got it. We'll keep an eye on it until you're able to be up and around."

"Well, but . . . I'll owe it to the doctor. Maybe you ought to give it to him now."

Grubb looked across the bed at the medical

man. It was Wolfert's turn to say something and Al was scowling him into it. As Wolfert bent to speak, Fred jerked his head. He and his deputies went silently out of the room and on out of the house.

"So it wasn't any hunter," stated Marshal Nolan.

Al growled: "Hell, you never believed it was. Let's go get the horses and have a look around out there."

"You and Bill go have a look," said Nolan. "I've got another little idea to check out."

"What idea?" Grubb asked, but Nolan didn't answer, he simply turned and walked southward as far as Elisha Wilson's harness shop, where he turned in, and caught the casual, steely glance of a man leaning upon the counter talking with Elisha. It was Con Wheeler.

Wheeler straightened up off the counter and smiled. "We meet again," he stated. "Well, I was leavin' anyway, Marshal."

"Not because of me, Mister Wheeler," purred Fred Nolan. "Elisha, you got my saddle finished yet?"

"No, Fred. I told you tonight . . . if I wasn't rushed."

Nolan looked on over where Delia was making what appeared to be a list of items to be replaced from depleted stocks, and, with his eyes on the lovely girl, said: "Elisha, you haven't had repair work on any Texas saddles or harness the last couple of days by any chance, have you?"

Con Wheeler and Elisha Wilson put owlish stares upon the marshal, as though both suspected this was no routine or idle question.

Elisha said: "As a matter of fact I did, Marshal. Patched up two saddle skirts and a busted headstall." He shifted to gesture over where a badly worn team harness lay in a heap upon the floor. "That harness is from the same crew of Texans. They left it here yesterday to have some fresh britchin' straps sewed on, and also to have a tug replaced."

"That's handy," Fred said, and drifted his glance on around to Con Wheeler. "You couldn't hardly expect fellows dragging a chuckwagon with 'em to pull out until after their harness had been repaired, could you?"

Con, catching the drift of Nolan's thoughts, smiled ironically and wagged his head back and forth. "Of course not, Marshal. Of course not. If you're finished in here, maybe we could go up to your office and have a cup of coffee together. Deadwood's dull as a cemetery durin' the day."

Nolan turned to precede Con Wheeler out of the shop. He had almost reached the door when Delia called softly to him from over behind the big workbench.

"Marshal, how is Gitalong?"

Fred turned back, a grave look on his face.

"Not too good," he said. "Where did you hear he'd been hurt?"

The girl came across to lean on the counter beside her father. "Everyone's heard," she said. "Marshal, can I go up and see him?"

Fred looked at Elisha when he answered. "Sure, Delia. In fact I think that's exactly the medicine he needs."

He and Con Wheeler walked outside and struck out for the jailhouse. On the way the shorter, stockier, and older man said: "Pretty girl. Prettiest in town, in fact. I'm surprised her father lets her stay in a place like Deadwood."

Fred looked down his nose. "It'd go hard with any man who talked rough around Delia, Mister Wheeler. She's sort of the mascot of most of us single fellows here."

Wheeler said no more until, in front of the jailhouse when Nolan reached for the latch, he halted and looked up at the lawman. "I reckon our minds work along the same lines, Mister Nolan. Pretty much, anyway. That's what I was in the harness shop for, too."

"What, Mister Wheeler?"

"To see if maybe those drovers hadn't fixed themselves an alibi for hanging around Deadwood a few more days. And they have, haven't they? No one'd expect them to pull out with only one half of a double set of harness, or without their torn saddles and bridles."

Fred removed his hand from the door latch, placed both hands upon his hips, and gazed straight at Wheeler. "It's against my principles," he said roughly, "to ask personal questions of folks unless I'm making an arrest, Mister Wheeler, but I'm going to make an exception in your case. Just what is your and your brother's interest in this mess?"

Con Wheeler answered as though this inquiry had not caught him off-guard in the least. He said blandly: "Curiosity, Marshal. Pure curiosity." His smoky gray eyes crinkled around their outer corners with lines of shrewdness and wisdom. "Ez is out havin' a little ride. When he gets back maybe the three of us can sit down and have a talk, Marshal."

Wheeler turned and walked off leaving Marshal Nolan looking after him. He was still standing like that when Delia Wilson walked up.

"Marshal . . . ?"

Nolan brought his attention around, wiped out the scowl which had settled across his upper features, and waited.

"After you left with that man my father and I had a little discussion. You see, he asked almost the identical questions you asked, before you came into the shop. We are wondering if perhaps there isn't something wrong. I mean . . . about what happened to Gitalong this morning. You know there is a rumor going around that

Gitalong was threatened last night by some drovers."

"You figure that fellow I walked away with might be part of some scheme to hurt Gitalong?"

Delia nodded her close-cut curly blonde head. She was regarding Fred with a solemn and concerned look.

He smiled at her. "It's the other way around, honey," he explained. "That man and his brother even agreed to pay Gitalong's medical expenses."

"Why, Marshal . . . why should two absolute strangers do that?"

Fred shrugged. "Well, I'd guess that maybe the Wheelers aren't as hard as they look to be." At Delia's puzzled expression, Nolan said gently: "Now you answer a question for me. I know you're Gitalong's confidante. I know, because I've seen him do it . . . I've seen Gitalong wait and watch for a chance to catch you alone. Now tell me, Delia, is it just pity you feel for him?"

The lovely girl's neck reddened. She dropped her gaze and was slow in answering. "Pity, yes," she said. "But, Marshal, have you ever taken a good look at him?"

Fred nodded.

"What would he be like if he didn't have that terribly twisted leg and wear those rags . . . if he wasn't starved half to death and if he somehow got a chance in life?"

Fred pondered what the kind girl had said. He

98

knew things about Deadwood and its residents no one else knew. He decided to do something which he ordinarily did not do—give a little private information. "He's a smart lad, Delia, and maybe with the chance you're talkin' about he'd amount to something. I'll give you something else to think about, too. Doc Wolfert reset that warped leg of his this morning. It was broken again in the stage wreck. Doc says, if he pulls through at all, that leg will be just about as good as new. Maybe he'll have a limp for a while, but it'll likely leave him in time."

"Oh . . . Marshal!"

"Wait a minute. I'm not finished. Delia, I don't figure it helps Gitalong's pride any to be called by that moniker, so suppose, when you go see him, you call him Neal."

"Neal? Is that his real name, Marshal?"

Nolan nodded. "Neal Duncan."

"Marshal," the lovely girl said breathlessly. "He never would tell me anything about himself. Do you . . . ?"

"Yeah, I know, honey. But it's not my place to say anything. It's his story. You understand?"

She nodded, her eyes unnaturally bright. "I understand. Marshal . . . ?"

"Yes."

She tipped up onto her toes and kissed Fred on the cheek, dropped back down, and walked swiftly northward up toward the Wolfert place.

The marshal stood watching her for long moments. He finally turned to hike into his office.

Al had left the Wanted posters in a mess after indifferently glancing through them for a description or a head-on picture which might resemble the Wheelers. Fred began re-stacking the pile. It was ungainly because he'd never thrown any of those old posters away, and several of them fell to the floor before he got the stack racked up. He sighed, bent to gather the fallen posters, and froze in his bent-over position as the face of the Texan who had died the night before in that gunfight stared back at him from a dusty old Wanted flyer in his hand.

John Petrie, the description said, was called Reb by his friends and was wanted in Nebraska for stage robbery, in Texas for stage robbery, and in Kansas for stage robbery.

No wonder Tevis Blankenship had been so bitter about Reb's killing.

Fred took the poster to his desk, placed it there face-up, sat down, and read the entire poster from top to bottom. There was a two-thousand dollar reward, one thousand of it posted by the Kansas authorities, one thousand of it posted by the governor's office in Austin, Texas.

He leaned back and gazed at the ceiling. The Wheelers had made a magnanimous gesture up there at Doc Wolfert's place when they offhandedly agreed to pay Gitalong's doctor bills. With a two-thousand dollar reward coming to them, they could afford to toss away thirty or forty dollars.

He brought his gaze down when Al and Bill walked in beating dust from their clothing. He didn't speak, just sat there, all loose and easy, waiting for his deputies to make their report.

Wentworth, heading for the water bucket, said: "The kid was dead right, Fred. There's a little dug-out in a sidehill . . . probably made by some gold hunter. He sat in there with his carbine and waited."

"How long was he in there?"

"Al and I figured maybe two hours, maybe a little less. He smoked three cigarettes and shifted position a half-dozen times."

As Bill gulped water, Fred and Al exchanged a look. Al said softly: "There's your answer about the kid bein' aboard the stage, Fred. That fellow didn't know Gitalong was on board. He couldn't have known it because he wasn't in town when the coach pulled out, and, also, he couldn't see inside the coach before he shot the horse."

Fred nodded. "Wheeler was right," he muttered, picked up the Wanted poster, and silently handed it to Grubb.

Al looked, looked closer, read the wording, and

as Bill returned from the water bucket wiping his mouth, Al handed him the poster.

Bill said: "Well, I don't believe it!"

In a way, Fred ruminated, this was funny. That poster was a clincher, or very nearly a clincher, about who in the Deadwood country was planning on robbing that bullion coach and how they proposed to do it. And yet, although Fred, his deputies, and even the Wheeler brothers had suspected this since the accident on the stage road, until that poster had showed up, there hadn't been anything but some pretty weak suspicions to go on.

Fred stood up. "Look through the pile again," he directed Al Grubb. "You saw the rest of Blankenship's crew. See if there aren't some more of them in there. If there are, we'll stop that robbery before it ever gets started."

Wentworth drew a shiny brass bullet casing from a vest pocket, tossed it upon Nolan's desk, and said: "That was in the hole where the bushwhacker waited."

CHAPTER NINE

Marshal Nolan left Wentworth and Grubb at the jailhouse going through his pile of posters, sauntered over to the boarding house to see the Wheeler brothers, and was told by an old man sunning himself in a rocker that the Wheelers had left not ten minutes earlier to get some supper.

He returned to the main section of Deadwood and began his search. There were at least a dozen little cafés, some no more than hastily erected tents with counters made of green slab wood laid upon wooden barrels, but there were also others of a more substantial kind. In the end though, Nolan went to that hutment café where the Wheelers had been eating when Blankenship's drover crew hit town, and it proved a good guess except for one thing—the Wheelers were not there.

They had been there though, Nolan was informed. Had left only moments before heading for Ace Morton's saloon. Fred turned on his heel and went up to the Bluebell. The Wheeler brothers were there, all right. They had a bottle of Monongahela between them upon a small table in the back corner where shadows lingered and where they had an excellent view not only of the roundabout large and barn-like room but also of the roadside doorway. They saw Marshal Nolan enter long before he picked them out of the shadows and threaded his way past the steadily increasing number of patrons.

Near day's end there were always the initial few who couldn't be bothered with supper and went directly to Morton's bar for their pick-me-up. This evening it seemed to Fred Nolan there were more of these dry-whistled men than usual. Even the poker tables had a few hands going. Ace Morton himself was sitting in at a fan-tan game with his coat on and with his back to the bar. He didn't see Nolan enter and, because he wore that coat now, instead of appearing in shirt sleeves, Nolan did not at once see Morton. Then, when he did, his lips unconsciously dropped a little. When Ace Morton wore a coat, the marshal had learned long ago, it wasn't because he felt a chill; it was because he had a shoulder-holstered six-gun and wished to conceal it.

The Wheeler brothers nodded and offered Fred a chair. He sat down, shook his head at the offer of a drink, and gazed at Ez Wheeler.

"You look like you're feeling all right," he said.

Ez impassively nodded. "Feelin' fine, Marshal." Ez's smoky eyes brightened. "Didn't know you were so interested in folk's welfare."

Nolan came near to smiling. "I'm not. But I am interested in where you went riding this afternoon."

Ezekiel openly smiled now. Even Con looked drily amused. "Went out and around," Ez said blandly. "Watched your two deputies find a little cave and explore it, then I sort of poked around the diggings asking questions."

"Come up with anything?"

Ez leaned back in his chair and shook his head. "No . . . at least nothing I wanted to know. I learned about rocker mining and sluice mining and placer mining, which didn't interest me one damned bit, but I reckon when you want some information from miners that's what you've got to listen to while you're scratchin' around."

"A wasted afternoon then," Nolan said, changing his mind and reaching for that glass and bottle.

"I wouldn't exactly say he wasted the after-noon," put in Con. "You see, Marshal, he went on down the river to within a short distance of the drover camp."

Fred, ready to toss off the drink, sat perfectly still gazing across at Con. He was obviously waiting for whatever else Wheeler had to say.

Con made a casual little gesture. "Drink it down, Marshal. Monongahela's scarce in Dakota Territory."

Fred drank, blinked his eyes at the fiery bite of that powerful whiskey, and pushed the glass away.

"He saw your friend over yonder in the frock coat havin' a long palaver with Tevis Blankenship and part of the Texas crew." Con turned his head to nod in the direction of Ace Morton.

Fred also looked over at Morton's coated back, then returned his attention to the Wheelers.

"That's why you boys are in here this evening," he said. "Wondering. Is that it?"

Con nodded and Ez reached for the bottle. Ez said: "Marshal, you got it figured about that stage pile-up yet?"

"I've got it figured," Nolan echoed.

"And this Morton fellow . . . where would you say he'd fit in?"

Fred didn't know. He knew Ace Morton, or at least he thought he knew him. Morton had come to Deadwood a couple of years earlier, about the time most of the other residents of the community had also arrived, right after the big hullabaloo about there being "gold from the grass roots down" had spread across the West like wildfire. But Ace had never mined. He'd opened his Bluebell Saloon, got financially involved in several other ventures around town, but had never shown any interest in the diggings other than catering to the needs of miners. Furthermore, although Morton was not a popular man and Fred, along with his deputies and others, did not like him, Ace had never been in any trouble with the law. Now he shrugged and told the Wheelers he had no idea where Morton would fit into any plan to rob the bullion coach.

"Not," he added, "that I'd say Ace was above it. Only that he's never given me any reason to believe he's involved with renegades."

Con and Ez exchanged that impassive but knowing look Fred had seen them exchange before. Then Ez tossed off his drink, as Con said: "Marshal, the stage-line manager told us his bullion coach will be in your bailiwick day after tomorrow."

Fred made a wry face without saying what he thought, which was simply that too many people were being too careless with their mouths about that coach.

Con understood and nodded silent agreement with this sentiment, but what he said jolted Fred. "This morning you asked me a question which I chose not to answer. But since Ez got back this afternoon and we talked it over, we decided it's time one of us answered the question for you."

Con reached inside his coat, brought forth a small leather folder, opened it, and slid it across in front of Marshal Nolan. There was a badge on one side of the folder and an identification card with a small photograph of Cornelius Wheeler on the other side.

"Pinks," murmured the marshal, and pushed the folder back across the table. "Both of you Pinkerton operatives, Mister Wheeler?"

Con nodded. So did Ez. Con returned his identification to his pocket and said: "You probably guessed it was something like that."

Fred smiled, leaned with both elbows on the table, and gazed from Ez to Con. "To tell you the frank truth," he said, "I didn't know whether you two were after the bullion yourselves, or after whoever else might be after it."

Ez chuckled and pushed the Monongahela toward Nolan. "That has happened before, too," he said, his eyes twinkling. "In fact one time we got arrested and thrown in jail over in Wyoming because we didn't identify ourselves right off."

Nolan ignored the bottle, looked thoughtfully over where swarthy, black-eyed Ace Morton was still playing fan-tan, and let off a long, audible sigh.

"Maybe there hasn't been a gold shipment that appealed to Morton before," he mused. "He's been here two years making money hand over fist in this saloon." He placed both big hands upon the arms of his chair to push himself up to his feet. "I'll have to do some fast checking now."

"To find out about Morton?" Con asked, and when Fred nodded, Con said: "Sit back down, Marshal. That won't be necessary. Ace Morton's no stranger to my brother and me. The first day or two we were in Deadwood we saw several familiar faces. Morton's among them. That's the main reason we also kept clear of you. If you'd been involved too, it wouldn't have been the first time a peace officer had decided he was being underpaid." At Fred's steady stare, Con shrugged and smiled. "Don't get mad, Marshal. You see, being suspicious of folks works two ways . . . you didn't trust us and we didn't trust you. Now, that's past. Now, whatever else turns up in this mess, we're more or less committed to work together to keep your coach from being piled up somewhere in a lonely spot like that practice coach was piled up this morning."

Nolan eased back in his chair looking from one of the Pinkerton detectives to the other. They in turn kept their wintry gazes upon him. "About Ace Morton," he said, bringing the talk back to that topic.

"He's been a lot of things, Marshal," related Con Wheeler. "Stage robber, rustler, professional gunman, filibuster down in Mexico, cardsharp . . . which is how he originally got his start . . . and gunrunner during the war. He's as cold-blooded as a snake, fearless, and as deadly a man with a gun as you'll ever come up against."

"He's wanted?"

Con shook his head. "That's the sad part of it. We know for a fact that he's been outside the law at least two-thirds of his adult life, but he's got no bounty on his head."

"Just how," demanded Fred, "did he manage that?"

"He's always been a mastermind . . . an organizer and director. But he's never personally led any raids."

Fred glanced over at Morton then back again. He reached up to push back his hat. This was more than just surprising; it was also very disconcerting. It crossed Fred's mind that Tevis Blankenship, if he was indeed involved in some scheme to attack the bullion coach, had eight men—nine including himself, and Ace Morton's hirelings at the Bluebell numbered another five rough, fight-scarred dealers, bartenders, swampers, and bouncers, which made a total of fifteen men—including Morton.

"Do you boys think he's in this with Blankenship?" Nolan asked.

Con shrugged. "Ez's report this afternoon makes it look that way, Marshal. But remember . . . Morton doesn't ride out, he plans and schemes and directs things."

"All right. Now then . . . what about Blankenship?"

"Well, we know him, too, but he's never been in anything like this before. He's been run out of Abilene and Kansas City for bein' a little too loose with his Forty-Five, and there are plenty of rumors that in times past he's picked up his share of strays on the cattle drives, but this is different. That's why we're sittin' back and waiting."

"Waiting for what?"

"For someone out at the drover camp to make a wrong move. For someone here in Deadwood to do the same."

Fred and Ez exchanged a look, then the marshal said: "Did you know that fellow they called Reb . . . the one who got himself killed . . . was wanted for stage robbery in Texas and elsewhere? There was a two-thousand-dollar bounty on his head?"

Ez nodded. "We knew. We didn't want that fight to come off and were ready to eat crow . . . to give him back his lousy three dollars . . . to avoid it, because we weren't certain that either Petrie or some of the other Texans wouldn't get a real close look, and remember having seen us before. Evidently that didn't happen though. Probably because it was dark over there in front of that café. Anyway, we've made it a point to stay out of their way since, just in case."

"And the reward," Nolan said. "What about that? In order for you boys to collect, the local law officer where Petrie was killed has to make the identification and the certification."

Con drew forth a folded, crisp paper from an inside coat pocket, tossed it carelessly down in front of Fred, and sat impassively while the U.S. marshal opened and read the paper. When Nolan's glance lifted over the top of the bounty claim, Con said softly: "Satisfied, Marshal?"

Fred was satisfied. The report was terse and factual, but what made Fred nod his approval was the name of the beneficiary who was given as recipient of the two thousand dollars: Neal Duncan, also known as Gitalong.

"Satisfied," said Nolan, thoughtfully folding the paper and handing it back. "Tell me, Mister Wheeler, how did you know that boy's name was Neal Duncan?"

"His father was a deputy sheriff down at Tucson in Arizona Territory, Marshal. He was one of those lawmen we spoke about a few minutes ago . . . the ones who sometimes figure they aren't bein' paid enough and go after outlaw gold. Ez and I are the ones who turned him in. He made restitution and left the country with his half-grown kid. We recognized the kid the same day we hit your town. That's what I meant when I said we found quite a few familiar faces in your town."

Nolan nodded. "Well, his pa's dead. Drank himself to death, gentlemen. When I was going through his effects I found the newspaper clippings from the Tucson papers."

"Does the boy know?"

Fred shook his head. "I burnt the clippings."

Con yawned and Ez, staring at the tabletop, came out of his solemn reverie to say: "We figure, Marshal, the kid's paid twice over for his pa. That two thousand ought to get him on his feet."

"Sure," agreed the marshal. "I knew there had to be something between the three of you when you boys offered to pay Doc Wolfert's bill."

Con made a little gesture with his hand.

"The kid did us a favor, Marshal. He acted as some kind of providence. Except for him being involved with Reb Petrie, and later, being on that piled-up coach, maybe we wouldn't have made as much progress as we've made." Con dropped his hand, considered its broad knuckles a moment, then in a quiet tone he said: "You ever wonder about things like that, Marshal . . . things like the son makin' up for the sins of the father, somehow, through ways folks can't really understand?"

Fred hung fire over his reply, and in the end he didn't attempt to answer the question, all he said was: "Boys, my name's Fred Nolan. Just plain Fred to you. I'm glad we had this little talk. Makes me feel like I've just had a good bath. Now about this other thing . . ."

"Sure," Con Wheeler said, also willing to let the abstract questions slide on by. "What have you planned for the coach?"

"My two deputies and I'll ride escort. We'll try and round up six or eight volunteers from among the miners or townsmen to ride along with us."

Con Wheeler yawned again, and inclined his head as he said: "Good enough. If you don't see us, Fred, don't worry. We'll be shagging along somewhere close by waiting for those renegades to make their strike. If we can prevent them from doing it, we'll do so. If not . . ." Con shrugged. "When the time comes, we'll be on hand to join in the fight."

CHAPTER TEN

Elisha Wilson caught Fred Nolan the following morning at the jailhouse with a worried look.

"Marshal," he said, "I want you to do something for me."

"Sure," Fred agreed. "By the way, did you finish my saddle?"

"Yes. I just hung it in the shed out back. It's now got spankin' new seven-eighths double rigging."

"How much, Elisha?"

"No charge . . . providin' you'll tell me something."

Fred motioned the saddle maker to a chair and said: "Shoot."

"It's about Delia and that waif with the crooked leg, Marshal. She came home last night after visiting him up at Doc Wolfert's place with starshine in her eyes. Now, Marshal, I want you to understand something . . . I'm not against the boy just because he's a cripple and a rag-picker. But you've got to realize Delia's my only . . ."

"Elisha," Marshal Nolan said calmly. "I reckon I can guess sort of how you feel, but I learned long ago the best way to fight a buzz saw is to stay clear of it. As for Gitalong . . . give him a chance. That's all, Elisha . . . a chance. Sure, he's dirty and ragged and honed down to skin and bone, but let me tell you this . . . he's fightin' back and when a buck with as many strikes against him as that boy has still comes fightin' back, he deserves his chance."

"What chance?" demanded the saddle maker, flinging out both arms in a wide and despairing gesture. "What possible chance does he have, Marshal? Listen to me. Delia's my only child. Since her ma died I've watched over her. Don't stand there and expect me to sit by and watch her ruin her prospects by gettin' involved with an unwanted waif like that."

Nolan bit down hard to hold his rising temper. He glanced up as Grubb and Wentworth strolled in off the plank walk. He said, forcing his tone to be even and quiet: "Elisha, if you want me to talk to Delia . . . all right. I'll do it."

Wilson stood up looking enormously relieved. "Thanks," he said. "I'm sure obliged, Marshal. She'll listen to you. Last night she told me you were the only person in Deadwood who understood."

"Elisha, wait a minute. I agreed to talk to Delia. I didn't say anything about interfering in her private life."

Wilson stood over by the roadside doorway, looking bewildered. Deputies Al and Bill made it a point to stroll over to the little stove and become very busy with the coffee pot.

116

Wilson said: "I don't understand, Marshal."

"I'll make it real plain for you," said Nolan. "I'll talk to Delia. I'll ask her to consider your feelings as well as her own. But that's all I'll do, because I believe Gitalong deserves a lot better from you than you're willing to offer right now. I also believe, within the next couple of weeks, you're goin' to have to eat crow about the things you're sayin' today. I'd advise you, Elisha, to be very careful what you say to your daughter about him, too. Sometimes the best meanin' parents turn out to be the biggest failures."

Wilson shuffled on out of the office. After he'd closed the door Marshal Nolan turned to look over where his deputies were soberly gazing at him from the stove area.

He growled at them: "Well, what're you two looking so hang-dog about?"

"Nothing," Bill Wentworth responded blandly. "Nothin' at all, Marshal. By the way, we just saw Blankenship and a couple of his lads buyin' supplies over at the general store."

Al Grubb's dark eyes and lowered brows were grave. "The pair of cowboys with Blankenship . . ." Al made a gesture toward Nolan's desk. "Turn over those facedown posters and meet 'em."

Fred swung around, saw the flyers, and reversed them. "Jack Younger," he read aloud. "Wanted for stage robbery. Bent Younger, his brother, also wanted for stage robbery." Fred twisted to stare at

Al and Bill. "Any others in the pile of posters?" he asked.

Grubb shook his head. "Not that we recognized anyway," he stated. "But those two ought to give you a sort of a hint, Fred, about who might've been tryin' out their technique on how to stop a coach full of gold dust."

The marshal sat down. He could of course walk over there right now with his deputies and arrest those two wanted men, and he thought, after a moment's reflection, that this is exactly what he'd do, but first he felt that both Grubb and Wentworth had a right to be brought up to date, so he explained to them about the Wheeler brothers, about Ace Morton's possible implication.

As he was finishing up, that anxious clerk from the stage company office rushed in to wave a slip of coarse yellow paper in front of Fred's face.

"It'll be ten miles north of Deadwood in the foothills come sunup!" exclaimed the clerk breathlessly, and dashed back out of the office, leaving the notice of the coach's arrival in Fred's hand.

Staring at the door, Al said harshly: "What the hell bit him, anyway, that he run off like that?"

Nolan studied the letter, tossed it aside, and crossed to his wall rack of rifles and shotguns.

"Come on," he snapped. "Let's take the Younger brothers. Maybe that'll stop things before they get out of hand."

118

● ● ●

But the three lawmen were too late. As they stepped out onto the plank walk they saw three riders loping northward out of town.

"Too far," grumbled Al Grubb, and swore. "Let's get mounted."

Fred vetoed this though. There were too many other things which now had to be done to chase Blankenship and the Youngers.

"Go round up some men," he said to Bill Wentworth. "Get at least ten if you can. As usual, the pay will be a dollar a day. Tell them to be here in front of the jailhouse by sunup tomorrow morning, armed and ready to ride."

As Wentworth walked off, Fred said: "Al, go hunt up the Wheelers. They might be at the rooming house over behind town. Tell 'em the coach is coming."

"Sure. Will they be ridin' with us?" Grubb asked.

Fred didn't think so. "I doubt it. Just tell them where we'll pick it up to start escortin' it on through our territory."

As Grubb nodded and started off, Doc Wolfert came up with a quiet smile upon his lips. "Good news," he said. "Gitalong's not only gaining strength, but the inflammation seems to be atrophying."

"Fine," muttered Fred Nolan. "Whatever 'atrophying' means." He turned to walk off.

"Wait a minute!" called Wolfert, rushing to stride along beside the marshal. "The harness maker's daughter was with him last night."

"I know it."

"She's the best medicine anyone could prescribe for the boy. He told me at breakfast this morning having her believing in him makes all the rest of it worthwhile."

Fred looked around with a scowl. "All the rest of what . . . gettin' cracked up in the wreck?"

"Well, I suppose he meant that, too, of course, but what he said was . . . it made him feel like a decent human being again. Made him feel that he didn't have to keep his identity a secret."

Fred halted and squared around. "What did he mean by that, Doc?" he asked, a puzzled look on his face.

Wolfert shrugged. "I'm not sure, but it had something to do with his father, I think. At least he mentioned his father."

Nolan stood like rock gazing at the medical practitioner. So Gitalong knew, had known all along. He'd probably run across those Tucson newspaper clippings before Fred had found them and thrown them into the stove, or perhaps he'd seen and heard enough before his father and he had left Arizona. Fred uttered a blunt curse.

Wolfert looked at him with a wide-eyed gaze. "Something wrong, Marshal?" the doctor asked.

"No, Doc, nothing's wrong. It just came over

me why that kid's never tried to get rid of that Gitalong moniker folks hung on him. I reckon, in his boots, I might have felt the same way. . . . Any name, even that one, was better than the way he felt about his *real* name."

"The girl called him Neal. Is that his correct name, Marshal?"

"Yeah. That's his correct first name."

"What's the rest of it?"

Nolan looked down his nose at Wolfert. "Why?" he asked acidly. "You figurin' on presenting him with a formal bill or something?"

"No, of course not. It's only that I . . ."

"Yeah, I know, Doc. It's only that you're nosy. Well, you just concentrate on bringing him out of it fit as a fiddle, and if he chooses to tell you about himself, that's his concern, not yours or mine."

Marshal Nolan walked away leaving Doc Wolfert watching after him. He crossed the roadway, hiked into the general store, caught the proprietor between customers, and asked what the Texans had bought.

The proprietor, a durably built, balding German with thick-lensed glasses pushed up now on his forehead, rolled his eyes in mock concentration, then said: "Bullets for Winchesters and Colts, hardtack, four sticks of dynamite, some flour, and some . . ."

"Did they say what they wanted that dynamite for?" Nolan interrupted to ask.

The German shook his head. "No. And I didn't ask," he replied. "They were hard-looking men, Marshal, and I'm only in business to sell, not to question."

"Sure," Fred growled, then walked back outside and almost collided with Ace Morton.

"What're you lookin' so black-faced about?" Morton asked, considering Marshal Nolan with his granite-like, jet stare. "Someone run off with your hobbyhorse?"

Fred's irritation was deep down, but it rose up a little now. He put up a thick hand and lightly tapped Morton on his thick chest. "Something I learnt as a kid," he said, "is that when a fellow feels like makin' poor jokes he always wants to be plumb certain the other fellow is ready to laugh."

Morton brushed Nolan's hand aside, his black eyes quickly flaring. "Yeah?" he snarled. "Maybe you're ready to laugh and don't know it, Marshal."

"What does that mean, Morton?"

The swarthy, coarse-faced saloonkeeper tapped his right shoulder. "It means that under this coat I got what it takes to back up anythin' I feel like sayin', Nolan, and that means if I feel like tellin' you to laugh . . . maybe you'd better laugh."

Fred, his annoyance unabated since seeing Blankenship and the Younger brothers lope out of town, felt all the old animosity for the dark and cruel-faced man before him come up in a rush. Without thinking, without speaking, he shot his hand out, caught Morton's coat, whirled the heavier man around, and gave the coat a savage downward pull. The coat, half-way down over Morton's biceps, hampered the saloon owner's movements. He could not, for example, reach under the coat for that shoulder-holstered six-gun. Fred then gave Morton a rough shove off the plank walk and out into the roadway. Morton, still hampered by that coat and unable for this reason to regain his balance right away, staggered ten or fifteen feet before he could swing around.

A dozen passers-by saw Morton out there, incongruously fighting to get his coat back up over his shoulders. They halted, nonplussed, to see what was happening.

When Morton got the coat adjusted again his face was black with fury, his cruel eyes showed points of fire in their lethal depths, and he started bringing up his right hand.

Nolan, his own right hand lying within inches of his hip holster, shook his head. "Don't try it, Ace, or I'll kill you. You've been askin' for that ever since you hit Deadwood. Consider yourself lucky that I didn't bust a gun barrel over your head in the deal, and next time don't talk so big."

"Next time," said the violently angry and humiliated saloonkeeper, "I won't open my mouth, Nolan. Next time I'll shoot first."

Fred eased off a little. He knew angry men, and this angry man was not going to make a fight out of it.

"Talk," he said. "Keep talking. It won't change anything, Morton, but it'll help you boost your sagging courage."

Morton, standing out there as stiff as a statue, almost choked on his next words, but he finally got them out, low and velvety soft. "Nolan, I'm goin' to kill you. I give you my word. I'm goin' to kill you!"

Several nearby men around Fred Nolan heard that threat, saw the thick, throbbing vein at the side of Morton's neck, and thinking the saloon owner meant to go for his gun, swiftly walked off to be clear of possible flying lead.

Marshal Nolan lifted his upper lip in a cold smile.

"You're free to try it right now, Morton. Or would you rather wait until my back's turned?"

Morton's scarlet features quivered with pure wrath.

Fred jerked his head sideways. "Go on back to your saloon. That's where you belong. And remember what I told you . . . be sure the other fellow's in a mood for laughin' before you try a joke."

Morton's black stare was venomous. He made no prompt move to depart so Fred deliberately turned his back and strolled southward where

Bill Wentworth was hastening up, having seen at least part of what had just occurred.

Wentworth kept watching Ace Morton. He desisted only when the saloon owner, with a violent oath, strode furiously northward toward his saloon.

"What caused all that?" Bill asked.

Fred shrugged. "I just wasn't in the mood for his sarcasm today. Well, how'd you make out with the posse?"

"Fine. Just fine. Got ten good men. They'll meet us in front of the jailhouse come daybreak."

CHAPTER ELEVEN

Al Grubb returned and said that he'd spoken to the Wheeler brothers. They'd assured him they'd be in the saddle and on the way before sunup the following morning. Then Al said: "Marshal, we got all afternoon. Why don't we head out there to Blankenship's camp and arrest those Youngers?"

Fred, still smarting from his encounter with Ace Morton, agreed to this. He and both deputies selected their Winchesters from the wall rack and went to get their horses. They got no farther than the livery barn where a fight between two huge freighters broke out just before they entered the place. Jeremiah Perkins came rushing forth. So did the liveryman, a small, ancient, and bandy-legged man named Buck. Andrew Jackson Buck.

Jeremiah spied the lawmen, dipped low in a curving rush, and sailed on up crying out that those freighters in the barn would demolish the place. Buck, sprinting in the opposite direction, turned, too, but his turn took him straight over to Morton's bar. He disappeared through the quivering doors in a swift rush.

Nolan quickened his pace. While he was still fifty feet away, he heard the tumult of that titanic struggle, and when he, Al Grubb, and Bill

127

Wentworth stepped around into the runway, they saw the battlers.

Both were very large, bewhiskered men, one fair and blond, the other dark and swarthy as though possessing Spanish or Portuguese blood. The darker man was back-pedaling to get clear of the oaken fists of his adversary. Al Grubb, usually the first one to rush in swinging, stopped, gauged those two giants—both well above six feet in height and over two hundred pounds in weight—and stepped to the convenient front doorjamb and leaned there. Bill Wentworth did the same. Fred looked around. Al caught that look and shrugged.

"They can't hurt much in here. Maybe spill some harness or a few saddles. Let 'em fight it out, Fred. I'll give two to one on the dark one."

"Done," Wentworth said immediately. "My five dollars is on the blond fellow."

The livery barn proprietor had not returned and Fred, who knew Andrew Jackson Buck quite well, didn't expect him to. Buck had a perfect excuse for tossing off a few over at the Bluebell. He was a man who never overlooked such an opportunity.

Jeremiah Perkins, nearly as large as either of those battlers but much younger, was aghast. "Stop 'em, Marshal," he croaked. "They'll bust something."

Fred stood still. The fair complexioned man he knew as a freighter who'd been hauling into

Deadwood for several years. He couldn't right now recall the man's name but he did recall that the man was usually cheerful and not the least bit troublesome. The swarthy man was a stranger to Nolan, and what he now saw of the man didn't meet with his approval.

The dark man had his fingers hooked like talons; he did not mean to use them as fists in the accepted fashion, but rather as raking, gouging spurs to tear flesh and dig into eye sockets. This style of fighting was not unusual on the frontier, but neither was it admired.

"Relax," Nolan said to Perkins, and followed up this advice by setting his legs wide in the doorless opening to watch the battle as his deputies were already doing.

The dark man was circling. He was bent forward in a menacing crouch as he sidled left and right looking for an opening. The blond man turned upon the balls of his feet, evidently experienced in this type of brawling, his left arm slightly extended to paw off his enemy, his ham-like right fist held back and high, cocked to strike the moment the dark freighter made his lunge.

Outside, behind Nolan and the others, men came rushing up, drawn mysteriously to the scene of combat although neither of the freighters was making a sound and both were midway down the barn's gloomy interior.

The dark man ducked and lunged. His adversary

struck like lightning with that poised right hand. The blow was high, glanced up along the swarthy man's cheek into his hair and knocked his shapeless old hat twenty feet away. The dark man jumped clear, shaking his head. A smaller man would have gone down from that blow but the dark man stayed clear for only a few seconds then bored in again. Now the blond man dropped swiftly down low, dug in his heels, and launched himself straight at his enemy. He caught the other freighter across the chest with that pawing left, heaved him off balance a little, and buried the right fist up to the wrist in the dark man's middle. Then he cake-walked sideways and stayed down until a sizzling overhand blow had passed fiercely overhead, after which he straightened up, dropped both arms, and savagely smiled. He had the dark man's measure now, or thought he had.

Al Grubb groaned.

Buck came pushing his way through the ring of intense onlookers. With him was Ace Morton and a dozen others from the Bluebell. When these boisterous men would have pushed on past, Marshal Nolan growled at them. Al and Bill also turned to scowl disapprovingly. The surging little crowd settled back.

Buck, a full head shorter than Nolan, craned upward and said: "Marshal, what're the odds?"

Nolan didn't answer.

The dark man scooped up a handful of dust and

threw it. His adversary merely swung his head, was showered with dirt, and swung back at the same time he executed a neat little prancing side-step, allowing the dark man to rush ahead pawing empty air. The blond man smiled again, and again dropped his arms waiting for the other man to come back around.

Al groaned again, and when someone jostled him, he turned with a snarl. Bill Wentworth was beaming powerful approval of the blond freighter. He stood to collect ten dollars, as things were going now.

But the dark man had his own bag of tricks. He came in cat-walking now, circling and pawing and weaving, his ebon whiskers framing sweaty features and coal-black small eyes full of venom. He feinted. When the other freighter carelessly walked into the trap, the swarthy man jumped at him, caught cloth in his straining hands, and hung on. Fred thought this would be the end, certain that once that dark one got his bear-hug set, he'd squeeze the lights out of the blond man. But it didn't work that way despite Al Grubb's cheerful curse. The blond man set himself flat-footed and threw all his considerable weight backward. Cloth ripped, the dark man was jerked violently forward, and out of nowhere an axe-handle fist exploded against the dark man's chest making his arms drop, making his knees spring all loose and watery as he stumbled backward.

The blond man was after him like a wolf, striking him over and over again between belt and collar, punishing the dark man with ruthlessness and science. The swarthy freighter moved instinctively to get clear. He turned to take that abuse along the ribs, to save his soft parts, but he was getting the worst of it now and seemed unable to fight away from the sledging blows that struck with a meaty sound as the blond man went after him no longer smiling and in dead seriousness.

The crowd behind Marshal Nolan loved it. Men hooted and twisted this way and that, living every second of the fight, feeling every blow, bawling encouragement to one or the other of those panting giants. The dark man went all the way across the runway, struck a stall upright with his shoulders making the building quiver, flung out a defensive arm, and knocked a set of chain harness off a wall peg. He tried to kick the harness forward with a desperate foot to entangle his adversary, but it was a fruitless endeavor—the blond man had anticipated it and stepped away.

Marshal Nolan saw the claret spew from the dark man's bearded lips where a blasting fist connected. He heard the dull thud as the swarthy freighter's head hit solid wood. Although the darker man would not go down, the only thing keeping him upright was the wall—that and his own bull-headedness. Fred raised his Winchester, started across, heard Al growl disapprovingly behind him, but kept right on going. When he was close enough he jammed the gun barrel into the blond man's middle, hard. This brought a gasp from the larger, fairer man. It also brought a howl of objection from all those blood-thirsty onlookers. But Marshal Nolan gave the barrel a second vicious push and drove the blond freighter back.

"That's enough," he said. "Slack off, mister. Your enemy's whipped. He's had enough."

Over in the excited crowd someone swore at Nolan. At once Al Grubb whirled, caught a skinny miner by his woolen shirt, and shook him like a terrier shaking a rat. Bill also turned, his brows down, his eyes smoldering. The crowd subsided.

The swarthy freighter, brokenly breathing and leaking blood from a smashed mouth, pushed up off Buck's wall, looked glassily around, took one tentative forward step, and fell forward to land face down in the rank dust of the runway. That ended it.

The blond freighter, his shirt ripped off, showed corded muscles that rippled under his sweaty hide. He gazed from Fred Nolan to the unconscious man at their feet, raised his battered right fist and blew on it. The knuckles were raw and red. He sucked in a great, deep-down breath of air and unevenly let it out. He turned, walked over near Al Grubb to lean upon the wall, and shake his head.

When he spoke, his voice, for the size of him, was incongruously high and boyish. "The damned fool. I told him there was enough haulin' for both of us. He insisted that we fight for it . . . all or nothing."

Fred lowered the carbine, looked around for Buck, found him, and said: "Any damage? Any charges you want to file?"

Buck shook his head. He was staring at the huge, unconscious man lying there in his runway, fascinated.

"Boy," he said to young Perkins, "fetch a bucket of water from the trough. Douse this one with it."

Bill Wentworth strolled over to Al Grubb and silently held out his left hand. He was gently smiling. Al gave him a spiteful glare and dug deep into a trouser pocket, brought out a number of crumpled bills, carefully selected two, and handed them over. He said something under his breath which Bill chose to ignore.

To the blond freighter, Fred Nolan said: "Who is he? Is that what it was all about . . . hauling freight into Deadwood?"

The blond man nodded, still sucking air. "His name's Gomes. I've run into him before on the roads. He's always been kind of rough-talkin', but, until today when we met in here, he never was really challengin'. Yeah, it was about the haulin'. But you see, Marshal, there's been a big new strike made east of here about twenty miles, over near LaPorte Butte. Someone over there found a nugget that weighed seven pounds. Pure gold, they say. Some other fellows opened up a vein two feet wide, also pure gold, and Gomes figured . . . the same as I did . . . that the freighter who hauled in supplies over at the new field first, would make a killin'. He asked me, when we met in here, was I figurin' on haulin' over there. When I said that's why I came to Deadwood empty, to load up right quick and make a fast trip to the new diggings, he said we'd fight for the franchise."

All those men standing out there in the lowering dusk were staring at the blond freighter out of round eyes. Not a man made a sound or even seemed to move for perhaps fifteen seconds. Then, almost as though at a signal, they whirled and went dashing away. Some yelled exuberantly as they ran, telling of the new gold strike. Others, less outgoing, kept grimly silent, but all of them, excepting Ace Morton, old Buck, the three lawmen, and one or two others who were not gold seekers, were off to throw together an outfit and race out of Deadwood in the direction of LaPorte Butte.

Fred watched them go. So did Al and Bill. None of these three attached any immediate significance to this exodus—not right then anyway. Al, ten dollars poorer, rummaged in his pockets for the makings and started to work up a cigarette. He would scarcely look at the blond freighter but when Jeremiah Perkins came up with a wooden bucket and unceremoniously emptied it over the swarthy freighter, Al nodded his head with bleak approval.

They got Gomes on his feet, got him able to navigate, then Marshal Nolan levied a curt assessment against him for a new three-dollar shirt. Gomes paid up without a word, shuffled off into the settling evening, and Ace Morton took him in hand, herding Gomes over toward his Bluebell Saloon.

Bill Wentworth craned at the gloomy sky. "Fred," he said to Marshal Nolan, "we'd never get down to that drover camp now before eleven or twelve o'clock. You reckon we still ought to go?"

Fred didn't think so because, even if they found the Youngers now, they wouldn't be able to return to Deadwood, lock up their prisoners, get any rest, and still be ten miles north-eastward of town by the time the bullion coach got into their territory.

"Forget it," he said. "We'll get some supper, snatch a few hours' rest, and leave town about midnight. Hey, Buck . . ."

"Yes, sir, Marshal!"

"Send your hostler down to the horse shed out behind the jailhouse for my saddle, and tell him to have our three animals rigged out by midnight tonight."

The liveryman nodded, his bright old eyes turning interested and strongly curious. "Sure thing, Marshal. You boys on a trail?"

Nolan turned his back on the liveryman, considered the huge blond freighter, and said: "Mister, where's your camp?"

"Three, four miles westward where there's good grass. Why?"

"Well, you head for it and you stay in it until morning. I've got a feeling Gomes isn't above sticking a shiv between your shoulders in the dark, tonight."

The blond man smiled and nodded. "Any stores open where a fellow can buy a new shirt?" he asked.

"Never mind the new shirt," stated Nolan. "You make tracks for your camp and pick up the new shirt tomorrow."

The freighter nodded and walked off.

Al and Buck and Bill watched him go, and at least the latter two of them showed strong admiration in their glances.

CHAPTER TWELVE

Al Grubb was gloomy until they reached the jailhouse again, then he said: "Marshal, Bill arranged for those posse men to join us a little before sunup. Hell's bells . . . if we light out around midnight, they'll all show up around here come dawn . . . and we'll be ten miles away."

Nolan considered this, found it logical, and went to his desk to sit down. "All right. On your way to your diggings tell the hostler not to rig out those horses until about sunup."

Grubb and Wentworth watched Fred remove his hat, cock his feet up onto the desk, and settle down deeper into the chair.

Wentworth, wearing a puzzled look, said: "Aren't you goin' to your room tonight, Marshal? You aimin' on sleepin' right here?"

"Anything wrong with it?" Nolan asked, looking around. "I've slept in a lot less comfortable positions than this in my life. You boys head on out . . . just be damned sure you're here before daylight."

Al rolled his eyes around at Bill, shrugged, and walked over to the door. As he passed through he put a wondering glance upon the marshal, then disappeared from sight. Sometimes it was hard to figure people out.

Marshal Nolan tilted down his hat brim and slept. He didn't bother barring the office door nor turning down the lamp, and as it turned out it was perhaps just as well because his slumber was interrupted twice. Once by Delia Wilson, and later by Con and Ez Wheeler.

When lovely Delia walked in looking unsure and hesitant, Marshal Nolan reached up, lifted his hat brim, squinted over toward the door, stared a moment, then settled the hat further back upon his head as he noisily cleared his throat and straightened up in the chair.

"Delia, you got no business bein' out this late at night, girl," he admonished her. "Your pa will fair skin you alive."

The girl closed Nolan's roadside door and leaned upon it. "Marshal, I had to see you," she said, almost spitting the words at him. "I visited Neal this evening up at Doc Wolfert's place, and as I was leav- . . ."

"Now listen here, Delia," Fred interrupted, his eyes studying her severely. "I think it's right fine you're cheerin' Gita- . . . Neal up, and all. But, honey, this isn't the hour or the place for us to have our little talk. And besides, a decent girl like you has got no business bein' out alone in Deadwood at this time of night."

"But, Marshal," she said, then frowned at him,

perplexed. "Our little talk . . . what little talk, Marshal?"

"Why, the one you and I are goin' to have."

"Marshal, you're not giving me a chance to say what I ran down here to tell you. As I was leaving Doc Wolfert's place I saw Mister Morton and a big, black-whiskered freighter putting some kind of powder in the grain barrels up at Buck's livery barn."

Fred and the pretty girl stared at one another for an interval of long silence. He brought his booted feet down off the desk with a solid sound, squared around in his chair, and was wide awake. He knew who that freighter would be. The same man the blond freighter had whipped to a fare-thee-well at the livery barn, and who Ace Morton had afterward taken so solicitously across to the Bluebell Saloon.

"What do you mean . . . putting powder in the grain barrels?" he asked. "What kind of powder, Delia?"

"I don't know, Marshal. All I know is that neither Jeremiah Perkins nor Mister Buck were there, and I saw Mister Morton and that bushy-whiskered big man dumping little sacks of some kind of powder in the barley barrels where Mister Buck keeps his horse grain."

Fred got up, no longer feeling the least bit tired. "Come on," he growled. "First we'll walk you home, then I'll go have a look at those barrels."

Nolan was heading for the door. Suddenly, Delia's discovery struck him like a physical blow, causing him to stop in mid-stride. All he could think was that Morton had poisoned the feed so that when the ten posse men Wentworth had lined up to escort the bullion coach gathered in the morning and then headed out, the horses would quickly collapse under them, if they even made it out of town.

He yanked open the door, jerked his head at the girl, closed the door behind her, and started northward toward the first intersecting roadway. There, without a word, he took Delia's arm and veered off as far as the fifth house down, where a parlor lamp was burning. He left the girl upon her own porch and retraced his steps as far as the alleyway leading up behind Buck's barn, turned in, and walked quietly along.

He was confident Morton and his cohort would not still be in the barn. Still, he was a cautious man under circumstances such as these, so he approached the barn's rear doorway silently, moving stealthily through the long shadows.

When he was in a position to look in, the runway was barren. He walked boldly up toward the front roadway, where a pair of guttering lamps hung on each side of the entrance. He halted near four wooden barrels with wooden tops upon them, and listened. Jeremiah Perkins was supposed to be around somewhere. Until he'd been standing in the total silence nearly a full minute Nolan didn't hear the snores because occasionally a drowsy horse would move in the opposite row of stalls, but when he finally did hear that noise, and determined it was coming from the overhead hayloft, he had his answer about Perkins.

He lifted one of the lids, picked out a handful of rolled barley, smelled it, made a face, and dropped the grain. Delia had saved him more than just a humiliating experience; she'd also saved his job, because if that bullion coach had been plundered while he and his armed posse men were walking back to town, carrying their saddles and unfired guns, the public uproar would have done the rest.

Now he knew what the Wheelers had meant when they'd told him that Ace Morton was the schemer, the organizer, and never the gun-wielding leader of an armed hold-up crew. He didn't have to do anything more than make certain no posse men could be recruited from among the townsmen, and when Jeremiah Perkins came sleepily down from his pallet in the loft to rig out horses for Deadwood's lawmen, he'd give each beast a good measure of grain to sustain the animals on—and that would be that—thanks to the careful plotting of Ace Morton.

Nolan went over to the harness room door, drew out a wired-together old chair there, propped it back against the wall, and sat down to do some cold calculating. Whatever tiredness he'd felt before was quite gone now.

Later, as the town got still and dark, he walked out as far as the livery barn front doorway and leaned there gazing across at Morton's saloon. The Bluebell was not only the most popular and best equipped bar in Deadwood, it was also the last one to close its door and douse its lights.

Fred considered walking over there, throwing down on Morton, and that black-whiskered big freighter if he was still around, marching the pair of them down to his jailhouse, and locking them up. He had half a mind to do this, when a pair of strolling silhouettes appeared along the northward plank walk coming down toward him. He couldn't make out the identity of those two until they were much closer, until he could hear their occasional quiet sentences as they came along, but neither could they see him in the heavy darkness of the barn's interior.

He let them get almost abreast of him before speaking their names quietly and brusquely.

"Wheeler . . . both of you. Step into the barn here."

Those two strollers stopped and turned, their faces mere circles of paleness in the late night.

One of them softly said: "That you, Nolan?"

"Yeah, it's me. Step into the barn here, I want to show you something."

They entered. Fred took them to the grain barrels, lifted the lids, and held up barley for them to sniff.

Con wrinkled his nose. "Strychnine," he said. "I'd know that bittersweet smell anywhere. We used to salt down buck meat for the wolves with it when I was a kid."

Ez Wheeler went to each barrel, lowered his face, and sniffed. When he was done, he looked around the barn, into the harness room, and finally gazed at Fred Nolan. "Let me guess," he muttered. "Morton's trick."

"A good one, too," Nolan commented. "To have me and my recruited deputies mounted on horses that would keel over tomorrow morning when we headed for the bullion coach rendezvous."

"Ahhhh," Ez said, and rolled his eyes around to his brother. "Morton's up to his old tricks again, Con. Reckon if there ever was any doubt about his being hand-in-glove with Blankenship's crew, there sure isn't now."

"No," agreed Con. Then he cocked a quizzical eye at Nolan. "How'd you happen onto this, Marshal?"

Fred made a small gesture of impatience. "That's not important now. I was on my way over to Morton's saloon to arrest him . . . and a big, Mexican-lookin' freighter . . . who put the poison in these barrels with him tonight. You boys care to come along?"

Con nodded. "Wouldn't miss it for the world," he said. But Ez hung back.

"Just a minute," Ez snapped. "Let's roust up the hostler who's usually around here, tell him what's in this grain, and put him to standin' guard over it. The stuff's got to be buried or burned. You can't just leave it like this."

Nolan went across to the loft ladder, climbed swiftly up, and called Perkins's name several times before he roused the hostler up. It took another several minutes before Perkins understood what was wanted of him and got sleepily dressed to climb back down to the runway where he rubbed sleep-puffy eyes and looked with amazement upon Marshal Nolan and the two silent men with Nolan, as it was explained to him about the poisoned grain.

As though he still wasn't sure, he raised one of the lids, poked his face down, and inhaled. He straightened up quickly making a face. There was a garrulous question forming on his lips when Marshal Nolan and the Wheeler brothers turned abruptly and walked away.

Deadwood's roadway was empty now except for a patient horse here and there along the hitch racks and an infrequent drunk making his leisurely way along. Moonlight filtered down through pale clouds giving the place an appearance of gentle decay and abandonment. Over at the Bluebell, lamps were still alight, but elsewhere, among the other bars and cafés, this was no longer so.

When Marshal Nolan and the Wheelers entered Ace Morton's place a weary and pouch-eyed barman was cleaning up. In one corner a passed-out cowboy endlessly slumbered, his head fallen forward on crossed arms upon a table top. The barman turned, recognized Nolan, and started to say something about the unconscious cattleman, but his voice trailed off into silence as Marshal Nolan walked across to him and halted. There was a look upon Fred's face that very plainly said the marshal was not the least bit interested in a drunk range rider.

"Where's Ace?" Fred asked.

The barman, with glasses from the roundabout tables in both hands, gazed from Nolan to the Wheelers, then back to Nolan again before he answered. "He left, Marshal. Him and another fellow. They left about an hour back."

"Where'd they go?"

The barman lifted his shoulders in an eloquent shrug and dropped them. "Dunno. That other fellow and Ace had a long talk, then they both got up and . . ."

"This other man . . . was he big and black-whiskered and dressed like a freighter?"

"Yes," stated the barman. "Marshal, what's up?"

Instead of answering, Nolan turned to cast a

sardonic glance at Con and Ez Wheeler. "Looks like this time you boys guessed wrong," he said. "Looks like Ace is going to take a personal hand in things."

"It'll be the first time, if he does," Con said, eyeing the bartender. "Mister, when your boss left . . . was he armed?"

The barman rolled his brows together as though trying to remember something. Finally, his face clearing, he said: "I couldn't take no oath to it, but he had his coat on, and usually when Ace wears a coat this warm time of year, it's because he's got a shoulder holster underneath it."

Con and Ez exchanged a look.

Nolan said to the barman: "Have you ever seen that dark-lookin' big freighter in here before?"

The barman wagged his head. "Couldn't rightly say, Marshal. They come and they go. After a while you get so's you don't pay no mind to any of them, unless, like that fellow over yonder, they pass out on you or start a fight or something."

Fred jerked his head and the Wheelers walked back out into the late night with him to halt upon the plank walk in the star-washed stillness.

He said: "You boys get astride and head out. I've got to wait around here for another hour or so until my deputies and our posse men show up. We'll meet you north-eastward where the main stage road passes down through the hills right about sunup."

The Wheelers departed without another word. Fred returned to the livery barn, and less than an hour later Al Grubb and Bill Wentworth showed up, carrying booted carbines.

The three of them talked a little about that poisoned grain, then set about leisurely saddling up. They killed plenty of time waiting for their volunteer posse men to show up, and finally, as the eastern sky was beginning to softly brighten, Fred let out a blistering oath. Al and Bill peered around.

"There won't be any escort," Nolan stated. "Dammit, why didn't I think of it before. That stampede last night for the new gold field. Hell, those fellows won't show up now at all."

Bill thought on this a moment, spat aside, wiped his lips, and said: "You mean it's just the three of us and those Wheelers to keep that coach from bein' hit, when we know damned well it's goin' to be hit by at least ten men . . . or maybe twice that many?"

Angrily, Marshal Fred Nolan got astride. He didn't answer, he simply said: "Let's go!"

CHAPTER THIRTEEN

They were a mile out of Deadwood when dour Al Grubb scowled and said: "Say, you fellows don't allow that talk of a gold strike over near LaPorte Butte could have been a trick to deprive us of our posse men, do you?"

Nolan had wondered about that back in town. First, a wild tale of a vein of gold two feet wide, twenty miles away, then strychnine in the livery feed.

"It could have been a trick," he replied to Al. "But if it was, it sure turned out to be a good one."

"Real good," muttered Bill Wentworth. "Probably fatal, in fact."

Al said: "Just how damned much gold is on this coach, anyway, that would get outlaws to make these elaborate plans?"

Nolan didn't know. The flighty manager of the stage office hadn't told him and he hadn't bothered to ask. Gold was gold, and in large lots aboard a special stage, it wouldn't be any negligible amount of ambulatory wealth.

"We'll never get a look at it anyway," he growled, "so why worry, Al?"

Al looked wry as he said: "No reason, I reckon. I'm just one of those old-fashioned boys who kind of likes to know just exactly what he's bleedin' about."

Bill Wentworth grinned.

They were passing into the hills now and as gently as that faraway paleness along the eastern sky had appeared, it now disappeared behind succeeding folds of lifts and rises. The stage road was still a short distance ahead. They'd made a short-cut cross-country ride to hit it near the long and continuous pass through which the bullion coach had to pass before it broke clear and began crossing more or less open country in the Deadwood vicinity.

It was gloomy and cold down in those swales and bottoms. It was also deceptively wooded and brushy. Fred Nolan, who knew every foot of this country, shook his head. He had, in times past, tried to interest the stage company in a more direct southerly route with its gold-carrying coaches, but the reaction had always been one of resistance. It was the law's job, said stage-line officials, to protect the coaches, not the company's job to seek out-of-the-way routes to minimize attacks and robberies. This had always struck Fred as a short-sighted policy, but when he'd said so aloud, all he'd ever got was cold stares from the stage company men.

So, the bullion coaches still came down through the passes, Marshal Nolan still rounded up armed guards to see them safely through his territory, and up until today, it had all worked out passably well.

But today—no.

He knew it in his heart, had known it the minute he coupled together that explosive story of the gold strike and the poisoned barrels which would not only have left Fred and his deputies afoot, but also would have put any belated posse of townsmen afoot who would have besieged Buck's barn for mounts when the news of the robbery reached Deadwood.

Well, if the strychnine scheme had failed, at least the other scheme hadn't, so here he was now, riding to escort the coach himself, with two deputies and two Pinkerton detectives, while riding to intercept, attack, and plunder the same coach were at least nine rugged Texans and perhaps Ace Morton and another man or two as well.

Bill Wentworth suddenly raised his arm, pointing dead ahead where three horsemen with two pack animals were coming up toward them on the same buck run of a little narrow trail.

"Miners," said Bill. "Headin' for Deadwood for supplies." This was a cogent guess—both those pack animals were carrying folded top canvasses and empty paniers, indicating their outfits were unladen.

Nolan selected a wide place in the trail,

stopped, and waited. Al used this respite to manufacture a smoke and hand the makings across to Wentworth. Fred, who didn't smoke, studied the oncoming men. This morning he would have been skeptical of the angel Gabriel, if Gabriel had been on horseback anywhere near the stage road in the Black Hills.

When the riders came up though, there was little possibility of them being anything other than what they appeared to be. For one thing they were rough, callused, weathered men with sluice mud still caked on their boots, and for another thing, although each man wore a belt gun and had a Winchester slung under his right *rosadero*, those weapons were old, battered, and dull with lack of care, definitely not the weapons of outlaws—even disguised outlaws.

The miners saw three men and three nickel-plated badges. Whatever their earlier thoughts or intentions might have been, those badges unquestionably made their strong impressions. The three men halted, sat impassively gazing across at Marshal Nolan and his deputies for a quiet moment, then each one quietly nodded.

The foremost man, whiskered and thickly made, spat amber, shifted his cud of chewing tobacco, and said—"Marshal,"—in a gravely unsmiling greeting.

"Where you boys from?" Nolan asked.

The burly man jerked his head backward. "Got

a camp about fifteen miles off. Got three legal claims."

"Anywhere near LaPorte Butte?" asked Nolan.

All three miners nodded at once. "Not too far from there," said whiskers. "You on the trail of someone, Marshal? We ain't had no murders or thefts lately . . . at least none that require you boys makin' that long ride."

"How about a big strike over there yesterday or the day before?" Fred inquired.

Whiskers shifted his cud and spat again. This time he ran the back of one hand across his bearded lips, dropped the hand to his saddle horn, and inclined his head as he said: "How did the word reach Deadwood so fast?"

Closely watching those three, Grubb exhaled, lowered his smoke, and exchanged a glance with Bill. So it was true after all; there had been a strike.

Whiskers went on speaking in his rumbling voice. "That's why us three lit out last night and pushed right along . . . so's we could get over here and load up before the rush commenced and those tarnal merchants got the word and tripled their prices like they always do whenever there's rumor of a big strike."

Nolan, for some reason he couldn't identify, felt enormously relieved, but it only took a moment of calm reflection for him to realize that, actual gold strike or pseudo gold strike, the net effect was the same. He knew everyone would be streaking it for LaPorte Butte, leaving the stage road, even leaving Deadwood itself practically deserted, and that meant Morton's plan had received a boost, planned or not.

He lifted his reins as though to ride on, but first he said: "You boys haven't seen a coach heading down this way, have you?"

The whiskered miner in his rumbling, deep voice said casually: "If you mean the bullion coach, Marshal . . . no, we ain't seen it. But some fellows we met up with last night said it had picked up the dust at three of the north-country camps yestiddy, so I'd reckon that'd put it somewhere down through the pass."

The miners nodded and rode on. Al and Bill twisted in their saddles to watch those plodding animals walk away.

As they squared back around, Nolan said to them: "Forgot to find out if they'd seen a couple of strangers ridin' up ahead somewhere . . . the Wheelers."

Al lifted his rein hand and eased his horse out. "That's understandable, Marshal, the look on your face when those fellows acted so indifferent about the bullion coach was almost funny. I reckon you were kind of startled."

"Shocked," Nolan admitted, resuming his way. "Stunned maybe, the way everyone knows about that damned coach. It beats me how everyone knows about it . . . where it's been, where it now is, and what it's carrying."

"You can't make the world over," opined Bill Wentworth. "As far back as I can recollect, folks in the Black Hills have been layin' wagers on whether the bullion coach will get through every summer, and so far it has."

"There weren't any Blankenships or Mortons around then," Al Grubb stated, killing his smoke atop the saddle horn and tossing it away as the stage road showed up far ahead looking like a pale, gray pair of evenly spaced ribbons cutting down through the crumpled hills. "And another thing, boys . . . if those Wheelers turn out to be somethin' we don't think they are . . . we're in serious trouble up to our scalps."

Nolan looked at Al. Grubb shrugged. "It could happen, Marshal. It's happened before. Fellows packin' all sorts of identification turnin' out to be somethin' else. I figure honey attracts the flies, and enough honey attracts the smartest flies."

"You're a cheerful devil," growled Wentworth.

The marshal said nothing. He had faith in the Wheelers, but then he knew them much better than Al Grubb did. It wasn't just their Pinkerton Detective Agency identification, either, it was the things they'd told him which rang true.

The trio came down through the hills to the roadway but did not pass out onto it. Instead, they kept parallel and higher up in the southward hills. It was a little like riding endlessly up and down, up and down, because each little spiked peak had to be ascended and descended, but it made good sense to do this even though it was hard on horses. They were always higher than the road, had an excellent sighting in all directions, and would in this fashion be able to see the bullion coach long before its driver and armed guard saw them. Also, it gave them every advantage toward sighting Morton—if he actually was along—as well as the men of Blankenship's outlaw Texas crew.

The sun was above the horizon now. It sprayed the uplands with a soft layer of golden light. Down in the cañons though, that same sooty night-time gloom still lingered.

Occasionally they spotted gray spirals of smoke standing straight up pencil-thin in the still morning air where miners had their diggings and their ragged camps, but almost without exception these were a long distance either to the south or west. All the slashes and scars upon the nearer hills around Deadwood had long since been worked out and abandoned.

There was no movement though, even as they passed farther north-eastward through the hills where the scent of oak smoke was a constant companion, but that was not unusual. Miners, with no urgency, worked their claims as they saw fit. It wasn't unusual for gold seekers to put off the hard labor each day until seven or eight in the morning, and it was now, by the marshal's close estimate, no more than perhaps six-thirty.

"This cookin'-fire smoke," lanky Bill Wentworth announced, "is makin' me hungry."

Nolan nodded. He knew how Bill felt. He rummaged in a saddlebag, brought forth a lint-encrusted, twisted, nearly black length of jerky, and offered it. Bill took the stuff and thanked his boss for it, but the expression of resignation across his long features made both Al and Fred grin.

They choused a bear out of a berry thicket near an upland spring, caught one glimpse of a wet snout stained blue from berry juice, a pair of astonished little black eyes, then the bear was gone amid a clatter of disturbed stones and the whip-saw sound of underbrush being charged through.

Where their ridge petered out, Fred halted, dismounted to give his horse a rest, and squatted with both reins in his hands. From this same vantage spot he'd watched for and awaited two previous bullion coaches. It was a good headland to survey the lower downcountry from. He had a clean sweep of the stage road for perhaps six or seven miles. He also had an excellent view of all the surrounding countryside, out of which a band of bristlingly armed horsemen could erupt at first glimpse of the bullion coach.

"Where you reckon they'll make their strike?" Bill asked, squinting down through the twisted arroyos and gloomy little cañons south of their headland.

"Anywhere," Al grunted, dropping down cross-legged beside his horse.

"Behind us," Nolan declared with certainty. "Somewhere behind us where they can hook the coach and drive it up a hidden cañon where no one's likely to find it for a day or two. Those diggings closer to Deadwood are abandoned. There won't be much chance of any outsider stumblin' onto them."

"Then what in hell are we doin' this far upcountry?" demanded Bill.

"We're here to sight the coach first and to ride down and go along with it. That's what we're doing here," stated Marshal Nolan. "What I'm curious about, is where those Pinkerton men are about now. I watched for their tracks all along and didn't see a thing."

"Over north of the road," suggested Wentworth, "cuttin' through the hills in that direction."

"Yeah," Al Grubb muttered dourly, "or else they've already met their friends, explained about where we'll be, and have got their blasted trap all ready to spring."

Nolan had no more to say. He traced out that

distant, sometimes sunlighted, sometimes hill shaped, gray run of stage road. It was empty as far as he could make out. Although there was no landmark, no tree or rock or depression in the land to indicate where he was supposed to pick up the bullion coach, he knew the exact spot. Still, as far out as he could see, there wasn't even any dust. Usually, he told himself, the coach should be at least in sight by this time of the morning. The idea flashed through his mind that perhaps other outlaws farther north had beaten the Morton-Blankenship gang to the gold, and although this was not a very commendable notion, he nevertheless smiled over it.

Then Bill grunted. "Dust upon the horizon yonder," he quietly exclaimed. "That'll probably be our coach."

Al sat straighter. Nolan, too, stiffened where he was squatting. Bill Wentworth had the best long-range vision among the three of them. It took another minute and a half before his companions also detected that lazy-standing gray banner. By then Bill could detect the racing coach just ahead of the dust, so he stood up, hooked his hands in his shell belt, and quietly nodded.

"That's the stage, all right," he said. "There looks to be four or five horsemen escortin' it."

Nolan arose. So did Al. Without any additional talk the three of them mounted up and started down off their hilltop toward the roadway.

CHAPTER FOURTEEN

It was still murky down in the cañons. Trees cast black shadows and the brush patches they passed through still held drowsy little birds who complained at this intrusion of their perching grounds.

The roadway, too, was blanketed in gloom. Nolan glancing up toward that three-sided headland they recently rested atop, saw how the sunlight was striking up there and estimated the time at near eight o'clock now. They had left Deadwood about four.

He led them out upon the stage road, turned left, and let his horse pick its own gait. They could easily reach the point of rendezvous ahead of the coach. They had only about a mile more to travel and the coach had at least five miles, so as they walked along, and the coach raced along, they should still reach the meeting point with time left over.

That's how it worked out too. They halted beyond the hills in the open morning lighted country, dismounted, and stood around waiting. Al had another smoke and this time Bill declined to join him, which was the only outward expression of tension Wentworth showed. Nolan turned to gaze out over the ten full miles of mountainous country they had just crossed. While the hilltops were sunlighted, the lower down brushy, tree-dotted slopes, as well as where the roadway twisted and curved through the cañon's only passageway, showed where that murky grayness still lay. It was that gloominess which, in his mind, was most menacing, because no sunlight would reflect off a gun barrel in that pass, or show a little puff of rising dust where horses stood stamping and fretting.

"Looks like near a half-dozen posse men ridin' with it," Al said, jutting his chin northward where the coach and its escort were now clearly visible. "Maybe we could talk those boys into ridin' on down into Deadwood with us."

Nolan didn't think so. For one thing the mounts those riders were astride had been running like that for many miles and couldn't keep it up for another ten. For another thing, this volunteer escort riding was never popular; once the men had accomplished their part of it, they turned back immediately. Finally, since that rumor of a big strike near LaPorte Butte was well abroad, these men had undoubtedly also heard it and would now be eager to get back.

"Hey," growled Al as he gestured to the north. "We got company. Look off yonder."

Nolan whirled. So did Bill. Two riders were coming out of a draw to the north that emptied upon the prairie perhaps a mile or slightly less, upcountry. The marshal let his breath out slowly.

"The Wheelers," he said. "Al, take my advice . . . trust 'em and don't act hostile."

Grubb shrugged, but he still kept his narrowed black stare upon the approaching riders, and his strong features were skeptical.

The Wheelers rode up, nodded, and stepped to earth.

"Nothing in the northerly hills," they told the trio, "and we take it you didn't run across anything on the southward side of the roadway, either."

"Nope," Nolan confirmed. "Nothing at all except the usual little breakfast fires . . . and three miners from upcountry who said that strike near LaPorte Butte is on the level."

Con Wheeler nodded, gazed up where the coach was looming large, and where its sounds began traveling far ahead of it. He looked around at the others and said: "Well, five to ten or fifteen could be worse, boys."

"How, I'd like to know," muttered Bill Wentworth.

Ez Wheeler, in the act of stoking a stubby little pipe, looked straight at Wentworth. "Easy," he said. "Did you know the outlaws had four sticks of dynamite with 'em?"

Bill sullenly nodded. "Yeah, Marshal Nolan told us."

"Well, Deputy, with five of us at least they can't

165

blow both sides of the cañon in some narrow spot and bury the lot of us."

"Why can't they?" demanded Al.

"Because," explained Ez, "my brother and I'll ride a half mile ahead all the way through the pass. We'll see 'em before they can catch the coach, and if they blow anything up, it'll have to be Con and me, which'll give you boys and the coach driver plenty of time to be warned, get the coach turned, and headed back out of there. That's why."

Al's expression, bleak and faintly hostile toward the Wheelers up to now, began to subtly change.

"You mean," he said quietly and very distinctly, "you two are goin' to ride ahead as bait?"

Con nodded as Ez finished stoking his pipe and lit it. "Unless you'd rather," he said, grinning a little.

"Get set!" barked Marshal Nolan.

The coach was beginning to slow, its escort riders rushing slightly ahead and deploying with drawn guns. Not, Nolan knew, because the riders didn't realize this was the rendezvous spot, but just in case the men afoot up there might not be U.S. Marshal Fred Nolan and his posse men.

They led their animals off the road and waited for the coach to ease down in front of them with a wisp of smoke curling up from each rear-wheel brake shoe. The escort riders halted. One of them, a short, wiry man stepped down, dropped his carbine into its boot, tugged off a glove, and walked up to Nolan.

As this man pushed out his strong hand he said: "Hello, Marshal Nolan. It's sure good to see you. I've never been as glad to get shed of a job in my life. There's more danged rumors of outlaws lyin' in wait for the coach than a fellow can shake a stick at."

Nolan shook the man's hand, saying: "Sheriff, don't suppose we could talk you into goin' on with us to Deadwood?"

The wiry man gave his head a sharp wag, turned, and pointed to the heaving, sweat-drenched horses of his companions. Then, gazing at Al, Bill, the Wheeler brothers, said: "You won't need us anyway, Marshal. You got as many men as I had."

Fred started to say something, but the wiry man had already turned and was walking to his horse. As he caught up the loose reins, he said over his shoulder: "There's a big strike over near LaPorte Butte. I got to get back."

He sprang up, saluted the armed guard and the driver of the bullion coach, waved his arm at his companions, and went rushing back the way he'd come.

"That," said Con Wheeler thoughtfully, "is about the fastest I ever saw an armed escort turn over its charge and depart. Funny thing about gold fever, it blinds men to the fact that they could darned easily lose all they already have in their pokes, while they go chasin' a rainbow lookin' for more."

Nolan walked over to the coach. The driver had climbed down to check his six-up hitch. He was a fiercely mustached, lean, blue-eyed man, wearing two tied-down .45s in low-slung holsters.

Before Fred could say a word, the driver, who introduced himself as Ryan, twisted to assess the approaching marshal, and he said: "You expectin' trouble in the pass?"

The marshal nodded. "Yes, as a matter of fact I am."

Ryan nodded solemnly. "If it's goin' to come, my guess would be that's the best place." He twisted further and looked up where the armed guard was sitting relaxed with a shotgun on one side of him and a Winchester carbine held between his knees. "You hear that?" he asked.

The guard nodded. "I heard it. You goin' to pet those horses all day or head on through?"

Ryan let his pale glance linger a moment longer upon the guard before facing Nolan again. He made a little wry face. "The company hired Parker there, not me," he said, speaking quietly. "They always hire gunfighters for these bullion coaches, and invariably they're about as companionable as a herd of tarantulas."

Al and Bill walked on up, along with Con and Ez Wheeler.

The driver looked them over. He seemed satisfied with their appearance. At least he said nothing about their limitation in numbers.

Studying Nolan, Parker, the guard, said: "Can't help but ask, Marshal Nolan, why, if you thought there might be trouble somewhere in the pass, you've come up with only four other men?"

Ignoring the irritable armed guard, Ryan said to Nolan: "I figure, unless there's a big swarm of 'em, Marshal, the seven of us can give a fair accountin'."

Con Wheeler said: "Driver, just how much bullion are you carrying?"

Ryan looked at Con. "Hard to say, mister. I go strictly by the weight my horses got to haul, whether its gold or passengers. I quit takin' any more weight on board when the frame got down to within three inches of the underside springs. That's how I limit a load." He glanced up at the scowling guard, then at the other. "If I was a guessin' man, I'd say there's probably . . . based on weight . . . close to a hundred and fifty thousand dollars' worth of dust and fine gold inside the coach."

Bill Wentworth's mouth dropped open. Al Grubb, evidently turning this astronomical figure over in his mind, gazed at Ryan as though he thought the man was either a fabulous liar or a mighty poor estimator of weights and values. Al just plain didn't believe any coach built could carry that much gold in it, which was understandable because Al, who had never in his life made more than thirty dollars a month, could not conceive of a hundred and fifty thousand dollars. Ryan might just as well have said a million or a trillion.

From the high, overhead seat that disagreeable armed guard said: "Hey, Marshal, you got any idea where we might get hit?"

Nolan shook his head as he looked up at Parker. "Somewhere between here and Deadwood is about all I'm sure of. As for how many, I'm figuring there'll be at least ten men in the gang, but there could be as many as fifteen or twenty."

The gunman swore.

Al, always a person of snap judgments and quick likes or dislikes, put a spiteful glance at Parker as he said, "Hey, when you're through cussin', I'll let you in on a little secret . . . they've got some dynamite sticks with 'em."

This alarming piece of information made the armed guard abruptly stop swearing and glare piercingly straight down at Fred Nolan. "Marshal, you mean to stand there and tell us for a damned fact you *know* we're goin' to get hit?"

"Yes," said Nolan.

"Then why in tarnation didn't you order them

fellows who come here with us to remain, why didn't you fetch along another ten or fifteen men, and why the hell didn't you comb this pass on your way up here?"

Nolan didn't answer that vehement set of questions. He simply stood there beside the resting horses, meeting the gaze of Parker. When his cold look had conveyed its disapproval to the man, he turned and said to the coach driver: "Deadwood's about emptied of men over the same gold strike that made your previous escort head right on back. This is all the men I could get . . . and they're all good men. But if you insist, driver, you can turn back. My job is only to escort you through my territory, south of town. I can't give you any orders at all . . . that's up to the stage company."

"Sure," Ryan said placatingly. "I told you my friend up there's got a disposition like a bear with a sore behind. Well, Marshal, the horses are rested, so I'm ready any time you are."

Con and Ez Wheeler turned to walk back to their horses.

Grubb, watching them go, said: "Fred, maybe I ought to ride on ahead, too."

Marshal Nolan shook his head. "We three'll ride with the coach . . . one on each side of it and one behind. The minute either of the Wheelers signal us, whether they holler or fire a shot or wave their arms, we'll stop the coach and get on which ever is the off-side from the Texans. Now let's get going."

Ryan went back down his hitch, stepped up onto the fore-wheel hub, and heaved himself up onto the overhead seat where he unwrapped his lines from the brake handle and waited until the Wheeler brothers were riding on ahead down through the gloomy pass. After that, Nolan took a position on the left side of the coach, Bill Wentworth took position on the right, or northward side, and Al Grubb took the flank position. When Nolan nodded, Ryan booted off his brakes, raised his lines, and the horses lunged, hitting their collars solidly to get the laden coach moving.

At once they left behind that pleasantly sun-lighted open country, moved down into the gloomy pass, and as the golden morning light winked out, their moods changed accordingly.

Parker, the armed guard, up beside Ryan, had his carbine in both hands now, cocked and ready to use as he constantly scanned the roundabout slopes and ridges.

Up ahead Con and Ez Wheeler were also riding with carbines athwart their laps, swinging their heads from right to left.

There was no way to make a swift run through this pass as long as the Wheelers up ahead held their mounts down to a walk. Once, when Ryan complained to Nolan about this, the armed guard growled at him, saying: "Let it go along like it is, driver. If some of these damned slopes are mined, and you run these horses, you could carry us right underneath a hundred tons of dirt and boulders before we could get clear."

Nolan, ever vigilant, nodded his agreement without comment.

The sunlight higher up was beginning to creep downhill as the morning advanced. Once, the Wheelers jumped a band of deer crossing from the north side of the road to the south side. The crashing run of these animals, about fifteen in number, put everyone's trigger finger on edge.

Another time, where some upslope animal jarred loose a small landslide of loose gravel, a half-dozen guns instantly swung to bear.

The pass got deeper and narrower the farther into it they went. Nolan went over in his mind's eye the place most amenable to dynamiting. The first spot would not be for another mile or mile and a half. He decided, before they got there, to call a halt and make a forward reconnaissance himself.

The team horses were fully recovered now from their earlier long run. They were walking placidly along taking an interest in the roundabout slopes, too, but without any of the same dread contained in the similar interest of the armed men.

CHAPTER FIFTEEN

The nerves of the men were taut after three miles had been traversed. Con Wheeler raised his arm to call a halt, which was roughly where Fred Nolan meant to leave them to scout on ahead anyway.

All five of the horsemen came together. When Ryan would have climbed down to join in their council, Marshal Nolan waved for him to remain up where he was, in full control of the teams and the coach.

Con Wheeler's face was shiny with sweat. Ez, sucking his little pipe which had long since lost its fire, looked to be under more strain than he could effectively hide.

Con said: "Marshal, as I recollect, from here on the pass gets narrower."

Nolan nodded. "That's right. In fact, within another hundred or so yards I was going to call a halt and do a little scoutin' on ahead. Now that we're stopped, I'll ride on. The rest of you stay back here."

Al Grubb immediately growled a protest, but Nolan cut him off with a scowl. When Ez Wheeler knocked the dottle out his pipe, pocketed it, and looked up and around, his brother said: "The marshal's right. We could afford to lose one man a lot better than we could afford to lose two or more. Besides, our first obligation is to the coach."

Nolan, agreeing with this, looked at Al and Bill. "If I fire a shot," he said, "you fellows close up around the coach because that'll mean I've seen something and can't get back right away. Otherwise . . . hang and rattle."

Giving the coach a quick glance, Nolan rode off, leaving the others to rest and give their horses a chance to browse a little. The disagreeable armed guard complained garrulously that it was dangerous sitting still like that down in the cañon where anyone could pick them off like crows on a limb.

"It's certainly not as dangerous," Al told the gunfighter, "as heading on down through the pass into some kind of a trap."

The sun was midway down the slopes now, which meant that high noon was perhaps no more than two hours away. The heat was building up, which was welcome to each of them, but up where Fred Nolan had cut into a game trail and was now passing steadily higher into the saw-toothed hills, the heat was stronger because, as soon as he left the cañon and got into strong sunlight, he was passing across land which had been getting the sun's direct rays since early morning.

There were groves of trees in almost every fold

in the hills where a scout for Blankenship and Ace Morton might be watching, but he had to run that risk on his way toward a top-out. Still, fortune favored him near the skyline. He came down into a little vale between two rough and brushy slopes where there was a tiny spring and perhaps a half acre of good grass in among some giant old stunted oaks. He left his horse here to browse, confident the animal wouldn't wander off or be seen, took his carbine, and crawled the rest of the uphill way on foot.

Where he came out the ridge was wind-scoured and barren. It was also gravelly so that each movement he made across it sent up crunching sounds. He kept just below the skyline and made a very cautious and deliberate skirting completely around the rimrocks so that he commanded a view in every direction.

And he saw them.

They were another mile or mile and a half down the cañon. Atop a slope which was lower than the one he crouched upon watching, sat a man with a steel mirror in his hand with which he occasionally signaled downward where Nolan could make out blurry movement from time to time.

The intended robbery site was about where he'd thought it might be. The road passed straight down between two nearly vertical cliffs of earth and rock.

It was one of the rare places in the entire pass where sunlight, when it struck, never lasted for more than an hour. If those two vertical slopes were mined with the dynamite the marshal knew Blankenship and Morton had, the pass could be filled with rubble from wall to wall within moments after the fuses were lighted. Or, if the dynamiters were adequately experienced, they could set off their charges, two in front, two a quarter mile behind, and forever seal the bullion coach and its armed escort in a steep cañon where, even if by some miracle, the men could claw their way out, neither their animals nor the coach could ever be removed without prodigious labor.

He went eastward down the land toward that rendezvous, managing to always stay well off the skyline. Though when he'd covered nearly a mile and had an excellent view of that sentry up there with his signaling device, he had to stop. In the first place, there was no longer sufficient protection to slip down any closer, and in the second place each onward step increased the perils of discovery.

He got into a clump of chaparral, lay prone and motionless for fifteen minutes, and tried to estimate the whereabouts and the numbers of those secreted men down there. In the end though, he had to abandon this idea because the hidden assassins did not show themselves. In fact, as time passed and the outlaws knew that the bullion coach had to be approaching their well-laid ambuscade, they confined their movements almost exclusively to watching their vigilante up there with his piece of polished steel.

But Nolan saw something that pleased him. He recognized both Ace Morton and Tevis Blankenship, the Texan, as they strolled up the empty roadway deep in conversation. After that, he eased himself back out of the chaparral and by extremely careful and time-consuming twisting and turning, got a sidehill between himself and the sentry up there with his mirror, before he dared jump up and trot back to his horse.

He was a full hour riding back where the others were anxiously waiting. The first man to spy him coming and say anything, was the armed guard high up on the bullion coach's seat.

"Here comes the marshal after his *siesta* up there in the brush," he called out. "Now maybe we can get this damned outfit rolling again."

Nolan was dismounting, handing his reins to Bill, when Al put down his Winchester, reached for the leather boot just below the coach seat, and started climbing. Al hadn't uttered a sound and Nolan couldn't see his face, but he knew Al, knew Grubb's low flash point. He whirled and hit Al with a sharp order just before Grubb could reach the armed guard.

"Get down from there, Al! Never mind him.

His tongue's goin' to get his head knocked off someday . . . but this isn't the day. I said get down from there!"

Al reluctantly climbed down. Until then, though, Parker hadn't realized how close he'd been to a personal attack. He now craned outward and downward to see who'd been about to lock horns with him. Al looked up. Those two exchanged a long, fierce glare, then Grubb turned and stamped angrily on out where Con and Ez and Bill were standing beside the marshal.

"Someday," Al snarled, shaking his head like a bull in fly time. "Someday . . ."

Knowing this was no time for infighting, Nolan ordered: "Forget it, Al! Now listen. They're on ahead where the hills stand just about straight up on each side of the pass. They've got a fellow atop a little knob with a reflector to let 'em know when we're coming. The others are hidden in the brush and rocks on both sides of the trail."

"Sounds like a perfect ambush," murmured Ez Wheeler.

"It is," Nolan stated. "Maybe we could run through, since the horses are rested and strong now, and maybe, the minute we hove into sight, they'd blast loose a thousand tons of dirt and shale rock, too."

Con Wheeler nodded. Anxious, he was listening very thoughtfully, and asked: "So, what's the plan, Marshal . . . sneaking up on them? Because if we try that, we've got to leave part of our crew here to guard the coach, otherwise some of them, sure as the devil, will try sneakin' around us to get the gold while the others are fighting us."

Nolan sighed as he lifted his hat to swipe at his brow. What Con said was indisputable. But even if it hadn't been, he had strong doubts about three or four of them making much of a showing against those armed and alerted outlaws down the cañon.

"I've got an idea that might work," he told the men after a couple of minutes of thinking. "It came to me as I was crawling through the brush to get back down here." He pointed to a brush-choked little arroyo off to the north which ran back up into a twisted fold in the roundabout hills perhaps a half mile before it petered out against a nearly straight-up hillside of weathered old rock and prickly underbrush. "We hide the bullion up there in the brush, then put our saddle horses ahead of the coach, loose, while we all pile inside with our weapons, and we run the gauntlet."

Con and Ez looked surprised. Al Grubb stroked his bristly chin while Bill Wentworth twisted to study the little brush-choked cañon.

"Man," Bill said, "I had a look inside that coach, Marshal. There's boxes and sacks piled in there that must weigh more than the five of us could pack if we were each twins."

"Seven," Nolan corrected, nodding toward the

coach where Ryan and Parker sat. "It's that, boys, or take our chances rushing through."

"Rushing through is out," Con Wheeler stated adamantly. "Even if they didn't have the dynamite, we couldn't rush past that many guns and not get stopped cold, Marshal. All they've got to do is practice their specialty."

Al raised his black brows. "Specialty?" he said.

Con looked sternly around. "You've got a mighty short memory, Deputy . . . shoot the lead horse and pile up the coach . . . then pick us off one at a time from ambush without losing maybe more than one or two of their own men."

Bill sighed. "Let's start hidin' that damned gold," he grumbled, and turned to go shambling back toward the coach.

They explained the plan to Ryan, and although he acted doubtful, he nevertheless got down off the coach to help. But the armed guard put up an argument. He was, he told them, getting paid damned well not to let anyone open a door on the coach or touch any of that gold, and he wasn't going to allow it now. To support this view, he put aside his Winchester, picked up the double-barrel shotgun, and pointed it at the men on the ground.

Con and Ez, standing off to one side, looked at one another. Ez said: "Mister Gunfighter, if you can add two and two, you ought to be able to figure out six to one. You so much as cock one barrel of the blunderbuss and six bullets are going to hit you before you can pull the trigger . . . mine being the first." He punctuated his words by sweeping back the coat he was wearing to make this threat real. Parker sat up there savagely glaring. Below him stood six armed men just as determined.

Into the silence that had lasted for a good half minute, Fred Nolan said: "Mister, I'm the U.S. marshal for the Deadwood territory. I take full responsibility for whatever happens, and that lets you clean off the hook, so put aside that shotgun . . . or use it . . . one or the other, because we haven't got any time to waste so we've got to work fast."

Parker put down his shotgun, leaned over to start climbing down, and he swore in protest every inch of the way until, squarely upon the ground, he turned and came face to face with Al, who scowled blackly, put up a battered, ham-like fist and shook it under the man's nose.

"You shut your damned mouth," Al said, "and start packin' those sacks and boxes, or I'm goin' to make your teeth into a necklace because I'm plumb sick of your belly-achin'."

Whatever Parker might have done under other circumstances—and he was undoubtedly not a coward or he'd never have been hired for the job he now held—his alternatives here were very limited. He'd made himself unpopular with every man around him, so he shifted, red-faced, went down the side of the coach, dragged out some keys, and unlocked the coach's door. He then re-pocketed the keys, reached in, caught hold of the first leather pouch, heaved it out, and went staggering around the coach toward the little brush-choked cañon.

The others followed this sterling example. Some of those pouches and sturdy boxes were so heavy they required two men to move them. Nolan encouraged the reluctant laborers to go farther up the little cañon with each load, using the sound logic that the farther they went the less chance of discovery was involved.

To this Bill Wentworth had some sound logic of his own. "Yeah, and when we come back for this stuff . . . if we're able to come back . . . we got just twice as far to pack it back down out of here, too."

They worked fast with little complaint even though they became scratched and torn by the underbrush. They got their chore done in something less than an hour, then, hot, tired, and out of breath, they went ahead with the next phase of their plan. They turned their mounts loose ahead of the coach to act as outriders, should it be the outlaws' intention to blow up the cañon ahead of the coach.

CHAPTER SIXTEEN

As they piled inside the emptied coach, Parker, standing outside and looking anxious, said: "Boys, I've heard of some hair-brained ideas in my time but this one takes the rag off the bush. You any idea what's goin' to happen to them horses when the gunfire starts up, down yonder? They're goin' to scatter like a covey of quail and leave the lot of us afoot up here with a herd of renegades a-bangin' away at us."

Con Wheeler, seated inside the coach with his brother on one side, Bill Wentworth on the other, warned angrily: "Guard, if I were in your boots, I'd be worryin' more about how small a target I could make myself up there on the box beside Ryan, because the first shots may be aimed at the lead team . . . but I'll give you big odds the second slugs are aimed straight at you."

Ryan came up and leaned his head inside. "You fellows ready?" he asked, looking from man to man.

Nolan nodded. "We're ready. And one other thing . . . look out."

Ryan nodded and grinned wryly. "I sort of had that in mind," he said. "The second I smell trouble I'm figurin' on loopin' the lines, settin' the brakes, and jumpin'. I've been fired on

185

before, up there atop a stage, and I can tell you it's a mighty uncomfortable feelin'." He leaned back a little, watching the Wheelers, the deputies, and the federal U.S. marshal check their firearms one last time, then he asked: "Any idea whether they'll blow us up or not?"

Nolan thought they'd use that blasting powder only as a last resort and said so. "Look for 'em to drop one or both your lead horses to halt the coach. If that fails, or if it looks to them like we're going to escape, then I reckon they'll seal off the pass ahead of us, but that's only a guess."

Ryan cast a final look around, stepped back, and started climbing up to his seat. Behind him, Parker, cussing with every move, followed him up. There was a moment of silence while Ryan gathered his ribbons, kicked off his brake, and got set. During that little relaxed respite Nolan looked at the others. They looked back. No one said anything, smiled, or even cracked a joke to relieve the tension. Neither did anyone look ready to abandon the plan.

The marshal said: "When we get down there, if you have to jump and run for it, remember that the Texans are up the northward slope, which is the only escape route, because otherwise the cañon walls are damned near perpendicular."

Bill screwed up his face. "Those walls are near . . . what?"

"Perpen- . . . straight up and down, Bill. A man

can't climb 'em and there's no cover, so if you have to run you'll have to take your chances up in the same thicket where Morton's men are also hiding."

Con Wheeler looked up. "Morton . . . ?" he said, looking dumbfounded.

Nolan nodded. "I saw him. Him and Tevis Blankenship together . . . talking out in the roadway."

Con looked at his brother. Ez said: "Well, for a hundred and fifty thousand I reckon Morton's finally decided to sit in on some action . . . for a change."

Al snorted. "Who wouldn't? We're doin' it . . . and we don't even get any share of the hundred and fifty thousand. I sure hope I get one straight shot at Ace though. Of all the cantankerous individuals around Deadwood, he's the worst, for my money."

The coach eased forward upon its springs, the teams picked up their tug slack, but they didn't lunge ahead as stage drivers ordinarily encouraged their animals to do. Instead, they simply began walking on down the road. Fred, seated next to the near-side door, leaned far out to see where their saddle animals were. Because the pass was narrow here and blocked on both sides by brushy slopes, the riderless animals moved along up ahead as though they fully understood what was expected of them.

Nolan leaned back just as Con looked at Ez and said: "Happy birthday."

The eyes of all three lawmen darted from one brother to the other.

Ez grinned at his brother, a tough, bitter little grin. "At least I'm ridin' not walkin'," he said. To the others he gave a little shrug and a philosophical observation. "Birthdays come and go. They never find a fellow exactly where he should be, but that's all part of life, isn't it?"

Bill nodded but the others remained motionless.

Each man had his Winchester, butt-down, upon the coach floor and gripped between the knees. These were not small men, so the coach was crowded. Al was perhaps the shortest and he was also the broadest.

Nolan leaned out again to check the saddle animals. "Still walkin' along up ahead like pack mules," he observed, bringing his head back inside.

Maybe a minute later, Parker sang out from above. "Hey, I just spotted a bright flash of light off somethin' up on a little knoll downcountry . . . maybe a half mile. Would that be the fellow keepin' watch?"

"It would," confirmed Marshal Nolan, again sticking his head out the window. "The others are below him and north of the road . . . up a little cañon. Let us know the minute you see anyone."

Con Wheeler, studying the steep slopes on either side of the hemmed-in coach, said: "Marshal, with the horses pokin' along like this there's a good chance they won't shoot the leaders after all. They could just step out and order us to stop."

Nolan nodded but had no comment to make. Speculation, this close to crucial action, tended to divert a man. Moreover, within a very few minutes now those outlaws down there were going to catch sight of five riderless saddle animals plodding along ahead of the coach, and be curious about that. He was certain that it wouldn't take them long to figure out that the escort was inside the coach, which would indubitably make them suspicious. Armed men only rode inside a coach under circumstances like these when they expected trouble and were set to meet it.

"Hey," Parker called softly down, his voice no longer gruff, only alert now and sharp-edged, "there's a couple of fellows standin' up out of the brush on the left side of the cañon right in plain sight. They're starin' at the saddle horses."

Nolan leaned to look out the window but he saw nothing. As he drew back, Con looked straight at him. "We better make a run for the cañon at the first shot, Marshal. If we don't, and if they have that dynamite set, they'll bury us sure."

Nolan nodded, eased forward to twist the door latch with one hand while he gripped his Winchester with the other hand. "Pile out on my side," he ordered, "and follow me up into the cañon. Don't bother returning any gunfire until you're damned well into the covert. Ready?"

Each man gave a quick nod.

Now Ryan called down, his voice gone thin and knife-edged. "Marshal, those two fellows smell something. One of 'em's run back out of sight up that little brushy cañon. The other one's standin' down there just starin' at them loose horses. What you figure we ought to do?"

Nolan opened the door, leaned far out, saw the easternmost end of the little brushy cañon, and replied: "Keep going. When I give the word set your brakes and jump off on the left side, and streak in up into that brush. We'll be right along with you."

At the precise moment that Con Wheeler leaned forward to say something, someone far ahead let off a yell which was instantly followed by an echoing gunshot. Con was hurled back against the seat as Ryan, not awaiting Nolan's order, looped his lines and leaped down off the left side of the coach. Parker made an indignant outcry as though Ryan, in climbing over him, had jostled the man. But seconds later, as Fred saw Ryan sprinting northward across the road, he saw Parker hit the ground and take off north, too.

Another gunshot sounded, this one farther up the brushy cañon.

Nolan kicked back the door and stepped down as he snapped: "Let's go!" A ripple of musketry greeted his emergence. One bullet struck the side of the coach, penetrating it and going right on through. At this, Al let off a startled curse and pushed Bill, who was ducking, out the door.

"Hurry up, consarn it," he grumbled at Bill. "It's gettin' full of bees in here."

That lone man down the road to the left, standing in underbrush to his waist, threw up a carbine and snapped off a wild shot before he dropped straight down. Ez Wheeler fired in the direction of the solitary man, then joined the others as they rushed for cover, leaving the coach abandoned and firmly halted in the center of the trail.

Understanding now what their foe men's strategy was, the outlaws, shouting back and forth, began to converge in a rush, evidently with the purpose of pushing the bullion coach's escort back out into the open where they could be finished off. But this came too late.

Nolan, with only his head and shoulders showing, fired his Winchester until it was empty into the underbrush up ahead. Con and Al Grubb did the same. This blisteringly hot fire drove the Texans into hiding, belly down, but their angry profanity rang out even above the thunder of the guns.

Ez knelt beside Nolan while the marshal reloaded, wagging his head as he commented: "Looks to me that these fellows are willin' to fight hard for that kind of money."

"They'd better be," Nolan said bleakly. "Win, lose, or draw they've got a battle on their hands."

Parker came slipping up and sank down to reload his .45. He was faintly smiling. It seemed that his disposition improved under stress. "They got to thin us out to get to the coach," he stated. "Marshal, why not let 'em get past?"

Nolan nodded, keeping his eyes locked straight ahead. "I was thinking the same thing. Once they leave the brush, the only shelter's the stage."

"Yeah," stated Parker, "and it's made out of wood. Bullets will cut through it like paper."

The words had barely left Parker's mouth when someone to the east—down where Nolan had last seen Ace Morton—shouted out to the hidden outlaws not to head for the coach, but to concentrate on driving the escort group out of their cover.

Parker's smile faded. He got up and fired down in the direction where the voice had come from. So did the others in the roundabout underbrush.

Once Ez's gun was reloaded he started off by himself, leaving the marshal and Parker together.

"Save your lead," Nolan snapped, as Parker paused in his firing. "He's not in the same place any longer."

Someone—Nolan thought it was Ryan—let off a high war whoop. This was at once answered by several of Blankenship's Texans with a Rebel yell. Gunshots slashed low through the underbrush around Nolan and Parker, who had left the spot where they had reloaded. They were now positioned in a little thicket-choked dip where they paused to gauge the location of the outlaws around them.

"No good," muttered the professional gunman. "You can't shoot what you can't see."

Nolan agreed, but added something to that observation. "It works both ways . . . if *they* can't see *us,* maybe we've got as good a chance as they have."

Parker looked around with a dark scowl. "Yeah? What we should've done was let 'em rush the coach."

The marshal gave the irritable man a steady stare. "Mister, in that coach we'd have been like sardines in a can. But that's not why I insisted on gettin' up into this damned brush amongst 'em."

"No? Then why did you?"

"Use your head," Nolan responded, ducking as a bullet clipped through the chaparral close by. "They've got that damned dynamite and whatever we do has got to be based on how they'll use it. They won't dare toss the stuff or blow up the pass as long as we're right in among 'em."

Parker's scowl slowly lifted. He gently nodded his head. Whether he liked Marshal Nolan or not, he was at least honest enough to say: "You're plumb right. I never thought of that. If they bury us, they bury themselves."

Nolan jerked his head and started off without another word. Parker dutifully fell in behind and trailed along. He seemed, in the space of a minute or so, to have changed his entire opinion of Marshal Nolan.

They crept to the end of their narrow little arroyo, slipped out of it, and at once ran into a furious burst of gunfire up ahead which drove them both down flat with their chins in the gritty dust.

Up ahead, a man began bawling for help, crying loudly that he'd come onto some of the enemy. This desperation-inspired outcry did not bring the outlaw the aid he wanted; it instead brought a veritable fusillade of lead into the underbrush where he was crouching.

Nolan heard the man cry out. He saw the brush up ahead shake wildly then subside. He and Parker exchanged a look, but they could not crawl ahead until that deafening gunfire slackened off.

When they were able to move safely, they found the Texan lying half in, half out, of a sage clump—his eyes growing dull, his body limp and slack. They eased the man around and shielded his upturned face from sunlight with their hats. The man gazed blankly at them. He was in shock, his eyes did not focus, and his lips softly quivered. He seemed to be trying to form the word water, but since neither Nolan nor his companion had a canteen they simply sat there, watching and waiting.

It was not a very long wait. The outlaw had four bullet holes in him—two of them were high up. He died with just a small shudder. Nolan leaned down to be sure, put his hat back on, and shifted to look Parker in the face.

"That's that," he said quietly. "Let's get out of here."

They crawled eastward, but got no more than a hundred feet before they ran into another blaze of gunfire from two outlaws who evidently had been converging on the spot where that dead Texan had called out from.

Parker ground-sluiced with his six-gun. He held the gun's butt down against the earth and swung the barrel from side to side sending bullets through the underbrush no more than six or eight inches above the ground. When he fired off his last round, Nolan heard those attacked men out there hastening away in a frantic rush to the east. He motioned for Parker to reload, not firing his own gun, and waited for his companion to complete the reloading.

He thought he had it fairly well established in his mind now about how the outlaws were positioned. In their initial rush down toward the bordering fringe of brush close to the pass, they had converged in a more or less even rank running from east to west. That dead outlaw had probably been the easternmost man of this line. Just about, because somewhere behind him and Parker, Nolan was certain either Blankenship or Ace Morton lay low where he'd seen those two before the fight.

Still, by cutting a short distance to the north while at the same time holding their easterly flank of that outlaw line, he was confident he and Parker had an excellent chance to relieve the pressure on their pinned-down friends over closer to the roadway.

As soon as Parker signaled that his .45 was ready, Nolan gestured to the north and started off again. If his guesses were correct, he surmised, they wouldn't encounter any more Texans.

They whipped back and forth through the tall brush, gaining confidence as they progressed because not a single shot was aimed in their direction. In fact, a lull had descended upon both sides, one of those little unpredictable interludes in battle which gave enemies a moment's respite.

Nolan used it by explaining to his chance companion what he had in mind. Surprisingly, Parker offered no objections. He simply listened and stoically nodded as he said: "Lead on, Marshal. I'm right behind you."

CHAPTER SEVENTEEN

They headed west in an effort to come down behind the Texans who were directing most of their gunfire at the coach's defenders near the roadway's edge. Parker was smiling again, a small, very faint and very lethal little smile. He had picked out the spot where a Texan was firing from. He looked over at Nolan with raised eyebrows. Nolan nodded and Parker fired. Someone let off a high squawk and the two could see movement in the underbrush up ahead. At once the other attackers paused to look back over their shoulders.

Nolan made a slashing motion and dropped down. Parker dropped too, and none too soon. Although Blankenship's cowboys did not know precisely where the shooters were, or how many there were, that didn't prevent them from sending a furious volley to their rear.

The marshal winced when a slug ripped into the sandy soil two feet ahead, showering him with dust and sharp-edged slivers of shale. Off to his left he heard Parker swearing as though it had also happened to him.

From down by the roadway another of those war whoops sounded. At once the gunfire from down there stiffened up into a ragged but angry fusillade. The situation for the outlaws became untenable since they were no longer facing just one line of fire, but two now, dividing their attention uncertainly between the enemy in front and the enemy behind.

Parker raised his head. Nolan growled across the intervening distance. Parker dropped his head again. For almost a full minute, flying lead, most of it too high, and undoubtedly some of it coming from their friends down near the roadway, slashed around them, but the moment it slackened, Nolan raised his six-gun and squeezed off three fast shots. Parker did better; he emptied his .45, then sank down swiftly to reload, grinning like a madman, his face sweat-shiny, red, and dirty.

The Texans divided their fire, but this time it seemed to Nolan they were shooting wild, shooting as though they were now fearful. He waited for the noise to subside again, then called out.

"You fellows on ahead there in the brush . . . this is Marshal Nolan from Deadwood. You're flanked. You can't reach the road and you can't get back this way, behind yourselves. Take a little advice and quit while you still can."

At once the unmistakable voice of Ace Morton called, sounding fierce, from east and behind Nolan. "Just keep him talking, boys, and I'll nail his carcass to the bushes for you." Morton emphasized that threat with a gunshot which was close enough to make Parker flinch and roll over onto his back as he tried to locate Morton.

Down the road someone evidently passed the word to open up again, and ragged bursts of gunfire began ripping at random through the underbrush. Nolan turned to say something, but his companion was no longer lying there. He squirmed around, guessing Parker had gone in search of Morton just as a bullet seemed to come out of nowhere and struck exactly where Nolan's head had been two seconds before. His muscles tensed as he sprang away. Then another gunshot sounded, another slug plowed into the ground. Without time to seek out whoever was behind him now, but guessing it had to be Ace Morton, Marshal Nolan squirmed and rolled until, in among some man-high brush, he could get up into a low crouch and run.

He heard his friends down by the road firing again. The outlaws too were joining that forward fight once more. It probably seemed to them that the attackers from the rear had been either killed or neutralized because neither Nolan nor Parker were firing at them any longer.

Instead of running farther away from whoever was relentlessly stalking him, Nolan turned northward, faded out into the underbrush, and waited with his cocked .45 tightly gripped and ready.

The heat was fierce in the pass now. Sunshine

was pouring straight downward from a brassy overhead sky. The gunfire began to dwindle a little, to become desultory, between Nolan's friends and their would-be robbers. He could see the stagecoach still up the road where it had been abandoned. He could even see some loose, saddled horses farther down the road picking at the roadside browse well out of gunshot range. It was an unreal scene—part pastoral, part deadly.

That stalking hunter didn't make a sound as he advanced. Nolan didn't see him until, when someone let off a howl down where the outlaws were hiding, a blurry shape spun half around, startled and tensed for action, barely discernible through some manzanita branches on Nolan's trail.

The man was not identifiable yet, but Nolan had him pinpointed. He raised his six-gun, waited for the outlaw to step clear of the manzanita— and fired.

The outlaw sagged, broke over in the middle, and staggered drunkenly, hard hit. The marshal cocked his .45 for the next shot, and waited.

That gunshot started the others firing again. It also brought forth another of those wild war whoops, only this time no Texan retaliated with a Rebel yell.

During this latest exchange the man Nolan had hit dropped his gun, threw out a hand blindly for support, caught only skinny little red-barked manzanita limbs, and sat down, his disengaged hand gripping his body midway between belt and collar. He lifted his hatless head, turned, and stared, his eyes bulging. Until he did that, Fred Nolan didn't realize he'd shot the leader of the Texans—Tevis Blankenship.

The lawman made a careful study of the roundabout underbrush, and seeing nothing to cause anxiety, he holstered his six-gun and took up his Winchester. Carefully, he moved over where Blankenship was grayly sitting with his jaws locked down hard against the searing pain.

The Texan looked up at him, his eyes swimming in anguish.

Nolan knelt, forced Blankenship's hands aside to examine the wound, saw at once that it was fatal, that the Texan was bleeding internally. He rocked back on his heels.

They exchanged a look, one questioning, the other gravely answering, but neither of them speaking. Blankenship read his death sentence and the muscles alongside his face bulged even as fresh perspiration popped out upon his upper lip and forehead.

"You never should have tried it, Blankenship," Nolan told the dying man. "Even if you'd brought it off, for that much money even the U.S. Army would've been on your trail."

"That damned . . . ," ground out the wounded man, pausing before he stated over again through clenched teeth. "That damned Morton . . . made it sound so easy. So clever the way he . . . had everything worked out. . . . The poisoned grain. The gold strike workin' right in to favor us . . . so you couldn't make up no posse. Everything so . . ."

"Take it easy," Nolan said, reaching over to throw one arm around the Texan's shoulders.

Blankenship bobbed his head up and down. Sweat was drenching his shirt now. The cords of his thick, bull-like neck stood out. "I wish . . . I could get my hands on . . ."

"I said take it easy," the marshal remonstrated. "He won't get away."

Blankenship's agonized gaze lifted. It was a wild, irrational, and glazed stare. "Marshal, get my boys to quit. . . . Tell 'em . . ."

Blankenship suddenly reared up against the restraining pressure of Nolan's powerful arm, strained half around, and threw all his remaining strength into one big bull-bass bellow to his men.

"Hey . . . you fellows. Stop firing. Quit shootin' at those fellows . . . with the coach. This is . . . Tevis . . . it's all over. Put down your guns. . . . That damned Morton got me . . . killed."

Blankenship's straining was hard to watch even for Fred Nolan who'd seen his share of men die hard. The Texan fought with every breath to cling to life, then he shuddered his full length, rolled his eyes back to stare briefly at Fred, and crumpled, falling forward, rolling sideways. Then he lay still.

Nolan heard a horse running, somewhere to the east. He ignored it to pick up his Winchester. He cocked his head to test the sudden depth of silence down by the roadway. He moved cautiously to regain his feet.

"You Texans!" he called out in a ringing voice. "Blankenship is dead. Stand up with your arms overhead. It's over." He paused, watching the brush quiver ahead as men hesitantly emerged into view, white and dazed and beaten. Also unarmed.

"Con!" he called. "Ez, Bill, and Al . . . go on up and check them for weapons. I'll cover them from here."

There were only five men standing up out of the brush. It didn't seem to Nolan that four had been shot, and, yet, when he recapitulated, he had seen one Texan get killed earlier and he was standing beside the dead body of Blankenship. It was very probable that his friends had accounted for at least another two.

When Al called out from in among the captives that all guns had been confiscated, Nolan walked down where the captives were being herded toward the roadway. He learned that two more had been killed, and one of the captives had been shot through the upper leg. That man was able to hobble along only because Al had unloaded a carbine and ordered the man to use it as a crutch.

Out in the roadway, Con Wheeler pushed sweat off his fiery face with one hand and held tightly to his Winchester with the other as he said to Marshal Nolan: "Where's the rest of them?"

Emerging a bit farther down, Parker spoke up ahead of Marshal Nolan. "I maneuvered a husky devil toward the east, jockeyin' for a clean shot, but he got a horse down there somewhere and lit out like a scalded cat."

"Morton," Al Grubb said explosively, and launched into a blisteringly profane denunciation of the Deadwood saloonkeeper which didn't stop until Fred Nolan ordered: "Cut it out, Al, and go get us a couple of horses."

Al turned at once and trotted off.

When Bill stepped up, Nolan anticipated what he was going to say and shook his head. "You help Con and Ez with the prisoners," he said before Bill could get a word out. Wentworth looked crestfallen.

The stage driver stamped out of the brush, knocking limbs and leaves and sandy earth off himself, while Ez studied the Texans, settling his eyes on the wounded one.

"You'll be Jack Younger," he said, then looked at the other captives. "Where's your brother?"

The wounded man spoke grittily through clenched jaws. "You fellows got him. He's back there in the underbrush."

Ez hoisted his carbine into the crook of one arm and started off.

As Nolan saw him starting off, he said: "Bill, go with him. You'll also find Tevis Blankenship along with another one back in there. Drag 'em out here, and if you boys will tie the dead ones across their mounts and go back for the bullion, Al and I'll ride on down the pass and hunt up Morton to make sure there are no more surprises planned along the route." He turned toward Jack Younger. "Where's the dynamite?" he asked.

Younger rolled his eyes. "That damned Morton had it. We was goin' to blow the pass and halt the coach with it. We also figured to drop one of the lead horses if you fellows tried running on past."

Al came up leading two saddle animals. He passed the reins of one beast to Marshal Nolan, turned, and mounted the other one and sat there, looking dark and grim but patient.

Ez Wheeler dug out his pipe, fell to stoking it and gazing at Nolan at the same time. "You be damned careful," he said. "If Morton's got that powder, he'll also maybe have the fuse or the caps to fire it with. You boys corner him and he still might blow you to Kingdom Come."

Nolan ran a testing finger under the *cincha* of the horse Al had brought him, which was not his own mount, stepped into the stirrup, and swung up. Then he nodded down at Ez. "We'll be careful," he stated. "Sorry to leave you with the mess."

Ez struck a match under one leg, puffed up a head of smoke, shook out the match, and dropped it as he said: "Don't worry about the mess, Marshal. We got two husky Texas boys who wanted to get their hands on a big wad of money. I sort of figure they've deserved the right, so we'll let 'em haul the cache back down from where we hid it and reload the coach." Ez nodded. "We'll meet you in town. Good hunting."

Nolan reined around. Al fell in beside him, still quiet, his face grim. As he and the marshal rode past the prisoners, Al turned a fierce look upon each of them. "If I had my way," he said to the group, "I'd hang the bunch of you to the first tree."

The Texans looked swiftly away from Grubb's savage glare.

Con waved from out in the brush where he and Bill were poking along in search of downed outlaws. Al waved back.

The deep, narrow pass was now full of piled-up afternoon heat and dancing layers of sun glare. It was also redolent with the residual stench of burnt gunpowder, and this smell lingered for a mile on down the cañon before Marshal Nolan and Deputy Marshal Al Grubb left it behind.

CHAPTER EIGHTEEN

They had no trouble picking up Ace Morton's tracks because the pass ahead was dusty and heretofore little traveled. Fresh shod hoof marks stood out clearly in the pitiless glare.

Al said: "He can go two directions, accordin' to my calculations, Marshal . . . due south and hope he can get out of the country before we overhaul him or straight on down to Deadwood."

"Why Deadwood?" Nolan asked.

Al puckered his eyes up into a shrewd expression. "One thing fleein' outlaws need more than guns and bullets is money. A man can't buy much protection from strangers with just his smile, Marshal. My guess is that Morton's got a cache of money at the Bluebell in town, and that he'll try almighty hard to get his hands on that cash before he lights out."

Nolan reserved judgment about this as they followed the fresh tracks of a running horse, kicking their own animals over into a loose lope, and heading straight down through the pass for nearly two miles before the tracks they were following abruptly swung off into the broken hills to the south.

Grubb made a grimace and looked up where the rims and ridges lay. "Looks like I missed my guess," he said, as they turned off to follow, but Marshal Nolan thought otherwise and said so.

"I think you guessed right, Al. In the first place, if he'd meant to go strictly south in his flight, he wouldn't have had to have come this far east before cutting through the hills. In the second place, the direction these tracks are going now, I'd say he's heading arrow straight for town."

They kept at it, pushing their animals when it was safe to do so and favoring them when it was not prudent to speed along. The tracks in front of them, though, never shortened in stride, not even when the trail led up through a stiflingly hot little shimmering cañon to a ridge, and led abruptly down the far side.

"The damned fool," Al swore disapprovingly. "He's going to kill his horse, riding like that."

Al had no idea, right then, how near to being right he was.

They labored up and over the skyline, plunged down its far side, and came into lesser hills and broader sweeps of open land. Finally, Fred Nolan raised his arm.

"Yonder, couple of miles ahead," he said. "That'll be our friend, and, unless my eyes are failing me, his horse is just about done for. Look how it's stumbling along."

Morton hadn't seen them yet and was concentrating upon his run-out mount. He was walking the beast now, but the damage had obviously already been done. Despite all the solicitous care in the world, the horse was physically exhausted, bordering on the verge of collapse, his rib cage pumping like a bellows.

Nolan and Grubb got down into the brushy country, passed from that in among some tree fringes, then came out upon the cured-grass tawny edge of a plain across which Ace Morton was toiling.

Al reined to a halt beside Marshal Nolan. "We can run him down from here," he said, carefully estimating the distance they'd have to first traverse.

Nolan shook his head. "He's still got that dynamite, remember. If we force his hand, he can bomb us with that stuff. On that played-out horse we can get plumb around him. Maybe we can even get between him and Deadwood."

They returned to the trees and began a long roundabout ride, sometimes loping, sometimes trotting, and sometimes just walking their horses, though it was a fast walk. It was a wearing ride, the kind to rub nerves raw in animals as well as men. It took them nearly three times as long to get completely around Morton, riding in their big circle, as it took the saloonkeeper to cover the same distance on his staggering mount. But they made it as the afternoon sun began to drop far down and color down to a coppery red glow which took the day's glare away entirely.

Behind them, visible but distant still, stood the tin roofs and square buildings of Deadwood. Elsewhere, close by, were the endless remnants, slag heaps, broken equipment, and gaping holes left behind by an earlier era of gold hunters.

They finally halted in a little stand of spindly pines within sight of the Deadwood stage road. Coming straight down toward them, still coaxing his almost wind-broke horse, came swarthy Ace Morton. From time to time Morton would twist to stare back up the slopes and along the ridges to the rear, but he didn't seem to comprehend that he could have enemies ahead of him.

Nolan stepped down, drew forth from its saddle boot his Winchester, handed his reins to Al and walked out twenty feet to a red-barked fir tree where he rested one shoulder upon the tree, waiting.

Morton's horse seemed to be recovering his wind. His step lost its wobbliness and he even raised his head a little to gaze on ahead. Then he pointed with both ears toward the stand of spindly trees and plaintively nickered.

Al Grubb swore as he watched the two.

Marshal Nolan froze where he stood, scarcely daring to breathe as Ace Morton, warned of other horses nearby in the gloomy place, yanked his mount savagely back on its haunches and grabbed for his Winchester.

To Ace Morton in his current difficulty, anyone

on horseback in among the trees ahead could only be a waylaying enemy. He hit the ground solidly, yanked the winded horse around, and lay his carbine across the saddle seat.

Nolan had no idea if Morton would fire. Neither did Al. Neither of them thought Morton could see anything dangerous in among the trees. But despite this, Morton fired, and if, as Nolan later surmised, he only did this to determine by startled movement whether or not anyone was in the trees, it was one of fate's little tricks that Marshal Nolan was destined never to know whether his surmise was correct or not.

Al threw himself from the saddle as a bullet slapped viciously into a pine less than four feet from him, and Al's horse gave a startled bound away. That was all the movement Ace Morton needed to see.

Nolan heard Al hurl a sizzling epithet at the horse from his prone position upon the ground just as Morton fired again, but this time he had his enemy located. Though intended for Al, the bullet drove Nolan to haul up sideways behind the fir tree.

Morton called forth a savage curse. His own horse, as lethargic as exhaustion had made it, fought to get away each time the saloonkeeper fired. Morton's aim was impaired by the necessity his desperate footwork required to keep the animal in front of him, which gave Al an opportunity to get up, spring over to where Nolan was, and drop down again where he had an excellent view of Morton. Al raised his carbine, dropped his head down, curled up his shoulder, and waited. The marshal, concentrating upon Morton's fight with the frightened horse, paid no attention to his deputy until Al fired.

The bullet evidently grazed across the rump of Morton's horse because the animal suddenly exploded into a bawling, pitching, plunging vortex of convoluting violence. Morton was hurled backward to the ground as the stung horse bucked and sunfished, head far down between both knees. The animal didn't stop bucking until he was a thousand yards away.

Morton sprang up and legged it frantically for cover behind a gnarled old oaken deadfall which lay upon its skeletal side. From behind this formidable bulwark he poked out his carbine and savagely fired three rounds into the grove where Nolan and Al were half hidden among the lacy shadows. Those bullets sang on through making their deadly high-pitched song.

Nolan dropped to one knee, took a long rest with his gun against the fir's rough and prickly bark and waited. Al, thirty feet farther off, abandoned his prone position and, like his boss, got behind a tree.

Fred caught a glimpse of Morton's shirt between the dun-brown grass and the fish-belly gray trunk of that old fallen oak. He drew a careful bead, let all his breath out to make the carbine rock steady, and fired.

For the smallest fraction of a second nothing happened. Then the entire forward world over by the deadfall exploded in a deafening red flash of blinding light and roaring sound. The tree went bodily up into the air, blew apart, and came down in large pieces. There was a terrible rushing of air into the vacuum caused by the explosion that almost sucked the hat off Nolan's head.

He was stunned. So was Al over behind his tree. Al dropped his carbine and fell to both knees, eyes bulging. It seemed to take Al longer to understand what had happened than it took the marshal. Somehow, some mysterious way that Nolan couldn't fathom, that bullet he'd fired had evidently struck some dynamite caps in Ace Morton's clothing, which had detonated and had, in turn, detonated those four sticks of dynamite Morton had been carrying.

For a full three minutes after the blast, while dust and small rocks were still falling back to earth, Nolan and Al remained behind their sheltering trees. Not until a silence descended, one nearly as terrible as that stupendous explosion had been, did Al grope around for his carbine and get back to his feet. By then Nolan was starting out across the intervening open stretch of land.

Smoke, or perhaps it was dust, continued to rise lazily up out of the crater where Ace Morton had been, and where now pieces of that rock-like old brittle oak deadfall lay scattered about for a hundred yards.

Where Morton had positioned himself, Fred halted, grounded his Winchester, and slowly looked around. There was no way of knowing that a human being had ever been in this spot at all.

When Al arrived at Nolan's side, all he could do was whisper: "Good . . . Lord. There's no sign . . . not one of him at all, Fred."

Nolan knew Al had said something, but he didn't know what, due to the unabating ringing in his ears. So he said nothing in response. He merely stood there, staring. Five, six minutes later, he turned and slowly went back to the horses. He pushed his carbine down into the boot, mounted up, and waited for Al. What had shocked him wasn't the explosion, although that had been bad enough because it had never occurred to him it would happen like that. It was the complete and total dissolution of Ace Morton, a man for which he had no sympathy.

He and Al rode out to where Morton's saddle animal was, caught it, and turned toward town. They rode silently for the first mile. After that, with most of the initial shock past, they talked some, neither realizing they spoke far more loudly than normal to be able to hear above the ringing in their ears. Around them the day was gradually ending. It had been a long day, a bitter day, and, in the end, a shocking day.

Deadwood was at that in-between hour when they came down the main thoroughfare. Most people were at supper. A few idlers stood by Morton's Bluebell Saloon and down by Buck's livery barn, watching the marshal and his stocky deputy ride past. At the livery barn, when Marshal Nolan turned in and whistled up Perkins to fling him the reins to Morton's animal, the idlers heard him say: "Turn the horse out, boy, Morton won't be using it again."

They left their own beasts, then gravely hiked on over to the hutment café, had a brief supper, and went to the jailhouse to wait.

A little over two hours later, Con and Ez Wheeler, Bill Wentworth, and the two stage company men arrived at the jailhouse.

Nolan cocked his head at Parker. "Who's watchin' the coach?" he asked.

Parker, helping Bill herd the captive drovers into the office, smiled blandly. "Ten fellows the local manager had lined up to do just exactly that while me and Ryan grabbed forty winks. Say, Marshal, I had you all wrong before the fight. I want to . . . ."

"Stow it," Nolan said, and he proceeded to

explain what had happened to Ace Morton.

The room of men stared at him, at Al Grubb, stared in disbelief when Nolan had finished. While this mood was on them, Bill jerked his head at Al, and the pair of them took the prisoners on through and locked them up in the steel cells. When they returned, Ez Wheeler was firing up his pipe while his brother was writing out something in longhand upon the edge of Fred Nolan's desk. When he'd finished writing, he carefully read what he'd written, nodded, and slid the paper across the desk to Marshal Nolan.

"You'll see that the kid gets it?" he asked.

The marshal picked up the paper, scanned it, and when he was through reading, he looked up at Con and inclined his head. "Be right proud to. 'Course I'll kind of appoint myself guardian and disbursement officer." He shook his head in wonder, adding: "That's a lot of money for a boy called Gitalong who's never in his life had a clean shirt nor a new pair of britches."

Con stood up and looked around the room at the other men before jerking his head at his brother. Ez joined him at the door. They both departed out into the lengthening night.

"I didn't understand all that!" Parker exclaimed from the chair in the corner where he had settled himself comfortably, his legs extended. "Are those two Pinkerton men, Marshal?"

"Yes."

"And they were sent here by the stage company to sort of keep an eye on the bullion coach?"

"Yes."

"Then why in hell did they just sign over all their Rewards to some punk kid called Gitalong? I always heard Pinks worked on a percentage or piece-work basis . . . sort of glorified bounty hunters."

Fred Nolan looked at Parker. "They had their reasons," he said. "Now you and your friend go get something to eat and then hit the hay, because, come dawn, we're off again for the last ten miles we handle to the south . . . out of my territory . . . with your coach."

After the two left, Al shook his head, blew out a long, rough breath, and finally said: "Even when he tries bein' sociable, I don't like that fellow."

Nolan stood up, yawning, before he let out a grin. "What say the three of us hike up to Doc Wolfert's place and see how Gitalong's makin' out?"

The trio was silent as they walked through the quiet evening. Without speaking about it, each had gravely watched the night barman go through the Bluebell lighting the lamps as they passed the ownerless saloon. Nolan, figuring he understood the thoughts of his deputies, broke the silence, saying: "Plenty of time tomorrow to take care of the details."

Bill frowned. "Marshal," he said, "you got any idea how many cattle are in that Texas herd?"

Nolan nodded. "I have an idea, yes. But we'll worry about disposing of them tomorrow, too."

Doc Wolfert met them at his front door. He put a finger to his lips, stepped outside, and closed the door behind himself. The lawmen turned still and apprehensively quiet. The way Wolfert had closed that door to keep them out had appeared to have a grim finality to it.

"Dead?" Bill whispered.

Wolfert's eyes widened on Bill. "Dead," he echoed. "Good Lord, no. Three square meals a day . . . and Delia Wilson . . . have done more for that boy than I ever would have dreamed possible."

"Well, then," Al growled, "why you keepin' us from seein' him then?"

Doc Wolfert smiled pleasantly. "Not right now, boys," he said. "Ahh . . . she's in there with him. I peeked in. . . ."

"Well," Fred Nolan demanded.

Wolfert's eyes puckered in a raffish grin. "She was kissing him."

The lawmen looked at one another.

Fred shrugged and made a suggestion: "Let's go have a drink, then come back . . . she ought to be through by then."

Al Grubb chuckled. Bill smiled broadly and dropped a sly wink at the doctor as they ambled off into the dusk.

ABOUT THE AUTHOR

Lauran Paine, who has written over a thousand books, was born in Duluth, Minnesota. His family moved to California when he was at a young age and his apprenticeship as a Western writer came about through the years he spent in the livestock trade, rodeos, and even motion pictures where he served as an extra because of his expert horsemanship in several films starring movie cowboy Johnny Mack Brown. In the late 1930s, Paine trapped wild horses in northern Arizona and, for a time, even worked as a professional farrier. Paine came to know the Old West through the eyes of many who had been born in the 19th Century, and he learned that Western life had been very different from the way it was portrayed on the screen. "I knew men who had killed other men," he later recalled. "But they were the exceptions. Prior to and during the Depression, people were just too busy eking out an existence to indulge in Saturday-night brawls." He served in the U.S. Navy in the Second World War and began writing for Western pulp magazines following his discharge. It is interesting to note that his earliest novels were published in the British market and he soon had as strong a following in that country as in the United States. Paine's Western fiction is characterized by strong plots, authenticity, an apparently effortless ability to construct situation and character, and a preference for building his stories upon a solid foundation of historical fact. *Adobe Empire* (1956), one of his best novels, is a fictionalized account of the last twenty years in the life of trader William Bent and, in an off-trail way, has a melancholy, bittersweet texture that is not easily forgotten. In later novels like *The White Bird* (1997) and *Cache Cañon* (1998), he showed that the special magic and power of his stories and characters had only matured along with his basic themes of changing times, changing attitudes, learning from experience, respecting Nature, and the yearning for a simpler, more moderate way of life.

Books are produced in the United States using U.S.-based materials

Books are printed using a revolutionary new process called THINKtech™ that lowers energy usage by 70% and increases overall quality

Books are durable and flexible because of Smyth-sewing

Paper is sourced using environmentally responsible foresting methods and the paper is acid-free

Center Point Large Print
600 Brooks Road / PO Box 1
Thorndike, ME 04986-0001 USA

(207) 568-3717

US & Canada:
1 800 929-9108
www.centerpointlargeprint.com